THE ELVES

DAVID S. SHOCKLEY II

THE ELVES
By
David S. Shockley II
ASIN : B00PZL405A
ASIN: 1503274527
ISBN-13: 978-1503274525
ISBN-10: 1503274527
ISBN: 9798364167798

CONTENTS

DEDICATION

For
Chloe, Skyla, and Summer Shockley
Aidan and Noelle Girard
Ellie and Ian Frenck
Kelsey, Gage, Blaise, and Raiden Silverman
Foster and Cannon Henby
Diver and Grace Davis
Logan Harris
Zoe, Noah, Kelsey, Campbell, Russell, Lulu, Emilie, Maddie, Emma-
Grace, Sydney, Winston, Maddie, Jackson, Aaron, Alex, Morgan,
Reyanne, Ava, Hunter, Zoey, Rebekah, Holly, Joseph, Gabe, Declan,
Jonah, Creighton, Josh, and Jacob

~A NOTE FROM THE AUTHOR~

When I was a child I saw an elf.

I was probably no more than five or six years old when it happened. I don't mean I saw an elf on television or in a book, or even on display at the various department stores where my parents shopped. It wasn't a picture, cartoon, or animated mannequin. I mean I saw an honest-to-goodness elf peering in one of my living room windows.

I've never forgotten that sight, though the rest of my early childhood memories fade as the years I stack on top of them grows.

We lived in Chattanooga, Tennessee at the time. My younger brother and I stayed at home with our mother, while my father worked. On this day, my mother was playing Christmas music over our family's only stereo, and I remember dancing about the living room in my pajamas. I was old enough to know that Santa was coming and that my parents were in a better mood than usual. The house was decorated with the few Christmas ornaments we had, and the tree we owned was one of the first I remember. At some point during that afternoon, I smelled cookies, though my mother wasn't baking. For one reason or another, I turned to look out one of the windows, and there he was.

The elf wore a green and white striped cap atop curls of bright blonde hair, had long pointy ears, and rosy red cheeks. He also sported a green and white striped scarf and crimson red mittens. He was laughing hard, which fogged up the window slightly, and just like that, he waved at me before vanishing in a shower of bright silver flashes tinged with deep gold sparkles.

When I raced to tell my mother, it was apparent to a child even as young as I that she did not believe me—though to her credit, she did tell me that the elf was probably checking in to make sure that we were being good. My little brother did believe me, however, and we were on our best behavior for the next half-hour at least! This was no small feet I might add.

I have never seen anything like that since, not outside of the magical realm of television or movies anyway. Could the elf have been the product of a young child's overactive imagination? Could he have just been a trick of sunlight? Could he have been a neighbor's child spying on the house next door? All of these things are possible, but in my heart I feel I saw an actual elf. And when he vanished that day in December so long ago, he took with him the wonderful smell of cookies that flooded my childhood home, but left me with a sense of magic that I have guarded to this day.

~*Dave Shockley* ~

CHAPTER 1

EYES IN THE STORM

J immy gazed at the silver and gold Christmas ornaments hanging above his hospital bed. Two reindeer-drawn sleighs twisted and turned in a soft glow of sporadic moonlight. Nurse Wilma had placed them there after he'd suffered a nasty coughing fit the week prior. He liked Nurse Wilma, or Willie as she liked to be called, and he enjoyed the decorations; they helped make the ward a little less scary, especially at night. Jimmy's mother placed some ornaments about as well, but the reindeer and sleighs were his favorite.

The third and fourth floors of St. Joseph's Hospital were reserved solely for children, though it was not a very cheerful place, not really. One might think a location filled with such young souls must be a happy, festive environment by nature, but not St. Joseph's. There tended to be more adults crying here than children, and Jimmy's mother was no exception. Most of the tiny patients shared a similar look in their tired eyes; a quiet and dim sort of light flickered where happier and brighter flames once danced. Jimmy's vivid blues were starting to show the same shadows, and the more time passed, the more he was okay with that. You can only fight so much when you're so young.

Jimmy understood that he was very sick. He also knew that his parents and the doctors, even Willie, were not admitting the whole truth of what ailed him. He could see it in their faces, especially their eyes. His mother's once brilliant blue-greens were now dull, flat, and almost as gray as the snow-burdened clouds which drifted over the hospital in recent days. Jimmy could always tell when his mother had been crying regardless of how hard she fought to conceal it.

His father was just slightly better at hiding his own sorrow, but he wasn't quite good enough to fool Jimmy. His letters home were always full of cheer and hope, but the way his mother skipped over certain sections when she read them aloud told Jimmy his father was indeed quite, quite sad. For several weeks now, the army had been trying to arrange transport for Jimmy's father so he could return home to be with his family, but correspondence had since become harder and harder to receive. Hitler's war-machine was intent on ruining Christmas for everyone, it seemed, even sick children half a world away.

It was the combination of tears, hushed voices, and quivering tones which hinted to Jimmy that he wasn't getting any better. He might feel okay from time to time, but despite his spirits, he knew something was terribly wrong. He was feeling less fine and less happy as more and more time passed. Part of Jimmy tried its best to battle the sorrow he felt growing in his heart, but there was also a tiny voice in his mind which whispered that being sad was okay. He didn't like that little voice, not one bit, but it was difficult to ignore, and it was persistent. No, there wasn't much fun to be had in the children's ward. But the colorful decorations did help a little.

Snow fell in quiet grandeur outside. Jimmy watched it with a small grin and thought of the times he used to play in the cool white stuff. Willie usually closed the curtains at night due to the chilly air, but Jimmy convinced her to let him watch the storm tonight if he couldn't sleep. She was reluctant at first, but ultimately left one of the curtains askew. His mother slept in a small padded chair near the window. When the moonlight escaped from behind the clouds and spilled into the ward, her skin would glow.

The chalky pills, vile liquids, and stinging shots Jimmy had been given earlier that day made him drowsy, but at the same time the medicines did ease his cough and the jagged pains which wracked his chest, so he endured them all without complaint. He had slept most of the day due to the drugs, and now he was finding it somewhat difficult to drift off again. A gust of wind turned the dark window bright white for a second, and larger snowflakes began to fall.

Jimmy wished he could sneak out and scurry through the fresh cold mounds. He'd do it barefoot if he could, even if just for a few minutes. A tiny cough and a not-so-tiny rattle in his chest reminded him that such capers might be ill-advised. His mother stirred at the sound he made, but soon drifted back into her dreams.

Across the room, a dozen or so beds cradled sleeping children, while next to them the occasional parent dozed in whatever chairs they had managed to procure, or a cot brought in by the staff. But one little redheaded girl in the far corner of the ward was still awake and singing about Santa. Her giant of a father half sat, half slumped next to her in a chair far too small for him. He snored as if he'd never get the chance to do so again and was therefore giving it everything he had. She and Jimmy had become fast friends in short order and though he didn't know too much about her, he did manage to learn a few things. First, her name was Jennifer, but she preferred Jenny. Second, she adored the color pink, as was evident in her nightgown, blankets, and pillow cases. Third, she loved anything to do with strawberries: strawberry ice cream, straw-

3

berry pancakes, even pictures of strawberries, which she drew, colored, and taped to various locations above the head of her bed. And fourth, despite losing her ability to walk or even feel her legs at all while here in the hospital, she never lost her ability to smile.

Jimmy knew that Jenny was going home soon; maybe even in time for Christmas. He would not be going home for the holidays, but Jimmy was happy for the little strawberry-loving girl none-theless. Well, happy *and* jealous all at the same time, so he didn't think of himself as too terribly bad, even if sometimes he wished it was him going home instead.

Jimmy sighed, muffled a cough in his pajama sleeve, and stared back out at the storm. The snow-laden clouds allowed the moon to inspect their progress for a moment, parting just enough to let the old silver orb peer down and cast its bright gaze over the earth. It seemed to approve of the clouds' efforts. They had done well in transforming the world into a white wonderland thus far. In the distance, tall, ice-capped mountains glistened in the night. Jimmy wondered how long it would take to climb one and imagined himself standing atop an icy peak in his pajamas, a hot cup of cocoa in one hand, a flag with his picture on it in the other. Mount Jimbo he would call it.

A moment later the moon vanished, taking the view of the mountains and Jimmy's fantasy with it. The snow began to fall even harder.

Jimmy watched the distance his eyes could penetrate into the cold night shrink ever closer towards the window. There would be a good amount of snow on the ground in the morning. He wished now more than ever that he could at least toss a snowball; maybe roll one down a hill. It might be good sledding snow, too. That would be even better. Whatever the case, Jimmy knew he wanted to play in it. What he did not know was that out in the storm, several pairs of eyes were looking back at him thinking the exact same thing.

4

CHAPTER 2

VISITOR HOUR

J immy watched the storm for as long as he could. Eventually, ice began to crawl across the cold glass as if spun of a thousand frozen spider webs. When the surface was too frosted for Jimmy to see beyond, he directed his attention back to the far less magical ward. Everyone was asleep now, even Jenny, the little strawberry girl who would be going home soon.

The massive room was awash in charcoal shadows, for which Jimmy was thankful. He preferred nights here in the hospital. The harsh fluorescent lights used during the daytime hurt his eyes and gave everything a sharp, intense gleam, so he always looked forward to the time when they were turned off in the evenings. During the hospital's most wakeful hours, the tile floor was almost always damp. The day staff was meticulous in their use of bleach and various disinfectants. Strong, pungent fumes would often burn Jimmy's nostrils and make his eyes itch. The cleaners were supposed to smell like pine, but to Jimmy they smelled nothing of the sort. By the time night fell, the astringent odors had usually dissipated. The sounds were friendlier at night, too. It was the one time Jimmy could hear whatever music the nurses played at their workstation, and the evenings were mostly devoid of coughs and cries.

In the far corner of the ward, a glass and metal office stood bathed in soft amber light. Inside, Nurse Amy sat at her desk reading a magazine while listening to a small wooden radio. Gentle Christmas music drifted out of the workstation and trickled over the ward. Jimmy thought Nurse Amy was probably the youngest of the staff. She seemed somewhat nervous around the sickest of the children, but this did not stop her from coming to Jimmy's aid whenever he needed her. She had a wonderful smile, freckles, and deep-brown eyes.

There were no cries now, none of the soft whimpering that often filled the sad room, and Jimmy was thankful for it. Not that he hadn't felt like crying himself on more than one occasion, but the sounds of other children, and especially their parents, sobbing into the night pulled at his heart, so he fought the urge whenever it trickled up into his own throat. He felt rotten already. Why make anyone else feel bad? Besides, his mother did enough crying for the both of them.

The ornaments above the bed twisted in an unfelt and unseen breeze near the ceiling. Jimmy watched the sleighs as the colored Christmas lights glistened and twinkled off their shiny surface. The sounds of the storm outside had increased, and they tried to drag Jimmy off into the world of dreams. They had almost succeeded when a strong scent of cookies tugged him back to consciousness.

Jimmy propped himself up and sniffed the air. Surely he had dozed off and imagined the smell, but after a moment, he wasn't so sure. The air was growing thick with the smell of cookies, all kinds of cookies! Maybe the kitchen staff was up earlier today? Maybe they were baking something special for breakfast? They did that sometimes, like the turkey and cranberry sauce for Thanksgiving. Jimmy took a deep breath and was almost overwhelmed by the aromas of cinnamon, ginger, cloves, and vanilla. He recognized all of these spices easily, as his mother used to quiz him when she baked, a game the two of them used to enjoy playing around the holidays.

The magical bouquet now floating about the ward was intoxicating. He glanced over to the nurses' station to see if Nurse Amy had taken notice of the scents, but she was nowhere to be seen. Another wave of sugary-laden air rushed across the room, and Jimmy's stomach growled for the first time in months.

He was about to wake his mother and tell her of the wonderful smells when an odd sound rattled up from one of the darker corners of the ward. There was a tiny clang, a dull clunk, and a metallic clink from the shadows. The odd clatter was followed by a faint "Oops!" and a soft chuckle. Jimmy peered into the dark and tried to see who had made the noise. Someone had entered the ward, that much was clear, but who it was, Jimmy was unable to see. A new and more pungent onslaught of cookie-scented breeze arrived, as did a figure at the foot of his bed.

"I didn't wake you, did I, Master Peterson?" the figure asked, and smiled.

Jimmy stared back at a large round man dressed in red and white and tried to speak.

"I should have sent you a letter, my apologies. I hope you will forgive an old man for his intrusion! But this is a very busy time of year, as you well know!"

"Santa?" Jimmy asked.

The jolly-looking man laughed and bowed. "At your service!"

CHAPTER 3

EARLY PRESENTS

When Jimmy was able to speak, his voice came out shaky and a little jagged. "I... I've always wanted to meet you!"

"Oh, we've met before! But you were very, very young," Santa replied. "You crept downstairs one Christmas Eve and caught me red-handed, so to speak!" Santa held up his crimson-gloved hands and grinned. "Well, red with white trim anyway."

"I did? I mean, you were? I...."

Santa chuckled. Aside from Jimmy, no one else in the room seemed to notice the ward's newest visitor. "I was mid-snack when you surprised me. Your mother makes some of the best hazelnut cookies I have ever tasted, since we're on the subject."

"She does?"

"Oh yes. It's been far too long since she has baked them, a travesty I intend to remedy!"

"You do?"

"I promise! If you will permit me, that is," Santa said, winking. "But where was I? Oh, yes! The first time we met. There I was, enjoying my second cookie, and in you walked! Just rounded the corner and took ol' Santa by surprise! You have to understand, it's a very rare event when I am caught off guard, much less on Christmas Eve. I dare say it's happened less than a dozen times in a hundred years! But there you were, standing in the doorway, eyes wide as snowballs." Santa began to laugh, rocking back and forth as he did. "I nearly choked at the sight of you! We had a grand time that evening, you and I. I promised then that we'd speak again one day. So here we are!"

"I wish I could remember that," Jimmy said.

"Oh, it will come back."

Jimmy looked over at his mother and then back out at the ward. No one paid any attention to the two as they spoke. "Am I... am I dreaming?"

"I should hope not!" Santa replied. "If you are, then I'm not really here, and that means I'm either behind schedule, or was sidetracked in some way."

"Behind schedule?"

"Well, Christmas is only a couple of days away! There's much to do between now and then, as you know."

Jimmy nodded. "So am I the only person who can see you right now?"

"Well, at the moment, yes. We wouldn't want to wake everyone, would we?"

Jimmy glanced back to his mother. "I wish my mom could meet you though."

"Little Suzy? Oh, we've met. She didn't surprise me like you did! But we're acquainted. Maybe I can tell you that story if we have time."

"Time?"

Santa walked over to Jimmy's side and ran his hand over the now frosted window pane. The foggy ice crystals on the outside of the glass vanished, and Santa stared out into the storm. "I have some friends who would very much like to meet you, Jim," he said.

9

"I promised I would bring them along tonight, and I always keep my promises."

"Friends?"

"Some of the elves, yes."

"You brought elves?"

"Actually, I'm not sure I could have come without them. They are a persistent lot! And that brings me to the reason for my visit." Santa looked down at Jimmy and smiled. "I would very much like to take you back home, Jim, home to the North Pole that is. The missus is keen to meet you, as are the rest of the elves. Oh! And the reindeer, especially Dasher. The two of you hit it off quite well!"

"Dasher? We did?"

"Oh, yes."

"I can come to the North Pole with you?"

"If you like. And don't worry about your mother. We'll be back before she wakes up in the morning."

Jimmy shook his head as if to clear it, grinned, and began to laugh. "I would like to see the North Pole very much!" he said, but then stopped and looked away. A shadow of regret washed over his features, and when Jimmy looked up again, several tears glistened in his eyes. "But I'm sick, Santa. I mean, I'm really sick. I'm not sure I should go."

Santa placed a hand on Jimmy's shoulder and smiled. "Don't you worry about that, Jim. Let's just say I have a few tricks up my sleeve for nasty coughs like yours! Helped bake 'em myself in fact!"

At that, Santa reached into his coat pocket and retrieved a large red and green cookie. "I'll tell you what; you eat that while I go up to the roof and ready the sleigh. If you aren't feeling better by the time I get back, then my name's not Saint Nick!"

Santa turned and hurried out of the ward. Jimmy sat in bed stunned, his head bursting with questions. Had he dozed off? Was he dreaming now? Could he wake up if he wanted to? Did he want to? Would he ever want to? He stared down at the cookie Santa

had given him and turned it over in his hands. It smelled wonderful. Red and green frosting was swirled around the top, and tiny
silver snowflakes dotted its surface. Jimmy took a small bite and
before he could swallow was positive it was the best-tasting cookie
he had ever tried. By the time he finished the last soft, sugary bite,
he felt better than he had in months—wonderful, in fact.

Jimmy looked over to his mother and contemplated waking
her. He wanted her to see Santa, to know that he felt better and
not to worry, but he did none of these things. Something in the
back of his mind told him to wait, that he would have a chance to
tell his mother everything later.

Santa returned after a few short minutes. His coat and hat were
covered in glistening snow, as was his beard. Nurse Amy was back
at her station, but she took no notice of Santa; she just flipped
through a magazine and hummed along to the Christmas tunes
floating about.

"Feeling better?" Santa asked.

Jimmy nodded. "Better than I've felt in a long, long time!"

"Grand! So what do you say? Would you like to visit the North
Pole with me? Stay for a while, have an adventure or two?"

"More than anything!"

Santa laughed loud at that. "All right, then. I brought you a new
coat. It can get a bit cold out there in the storm, but this should do
quite nicely."

Santa pulled an emerald green coat from a large red bag and
handed it to Jimmy.

"It looks almost like yours!" Jimmy said.

"Well, Mrs. Claus made both of them. She worked on yours for
a month straight!"

"She did?"

"Oh yes. But don't tell her I told you so. She gets embarrassed
easily," Santa said, and winked.

Jimmy climbed out of his bed and pulled the coat on.

"You might want these too," Santa said, and handed Jimmy a pair of black boots. "Now those I made. They're lined with rein-deer fur! Comet always donates the absolute best fur for boots."

"Thank you!"

Santa laughed. "My pleasure, Jim."

CHAPTER 4

ROOFTOP MAGIC

J immy pulled his new coat and boots over his pajamas. Santa complimented his choice of Lone Ranger apparel and tucked a large blanket around Jimmy's mother as she slept. It looked very warm and soft, and was decorated with silver snowflakes atop a cobalt blue background. When they turned to go, no one noticed them in the slightest.

"Nurse Amy won't find me missing and be worried, will she?"

Santa smiled. "Oh no, no, no, but you do bring up a very good point!"

He stopped and looked above the doors leading out of the ward at a large white clock. "Let's slow things down a bit, shall we?"

Santa retrieved a small silver pocket watch from his coat. He turned it in his hands and flipped open the crystal face. With one careful touch of his mitten, a shower of green and gold lights erupted from the timepiece. They hovered like tiny sparkling fairies, then raced up and into the clock on the wall. Jimmy stared in wonder as the second hand crawled to a stop.

"I think that should do it!" Santa said.

"You stopped time?"

Santa chuckled. "Oh no, I can't stop time," he replied. "But I am exceptionally good at slowing it down! You see?"

Jimmy looked back at the clock for a moment and was surprised to see the second hand was still moving, albeit now in a very drowsy and extremely sluggish manner.

"So no, I don't stop time, but I can ask it to do favors for me on occasion! Shall we be on our way?"

Jimmy nodded, and the two continued on. The hallway outside the children's ward was dim, but Santa held his pocket watch aloft, and it began to emit a cool blue light. It was just bright enough to see by.

"A gift from the elves," Santa said when he noticed Jimmy staring again.

"Does it do anything else?" Jimmy asked.

"Well, it plays quite a few melodies! It comes up with new ones on an almost weekly basis. I think it's something of a composer. The elves never cease to amaze me."

"Wow."

Santa chuckled. "I heard it singing off in a cupboard one night, but I can't seem to convince it to do so again. Maybe it's stubborn, or perhaps it's just shy. I'm not sure why though, as the voice I heard was quite a lovely one," he said, more to the timepiece than to Jimmy.

The trip up to the roof was easier on Jimmy than he imagined it would be. For a while now, the simple act of walking across the ward was enough to leave him breathless and aching, not to mention coughing and choking for a time. But tonight…tonight he felt as if he could have raced up a thousand stairs, then down, and back up again! The feelings put a cheerful skip in his stride and a genuine grin on his cheeks.

When they reached the cold metal door leading to the roof, Santa pushed it aside, shoving a sizable drift of snow behind it in order to squeeze out. Jimmy followed close behind.

"Now let me know if you start to get chilly!" Santa said.

Jimmy was about to answer when he noticed the snowflakes around them were no longer falling. In fact, they weren't moving at all! Instead, the little icy constructs simply hung motionless in midair!

"It does look pretty when you slow ol' Father Time, doesn't it?" Santa said.

Jimmy nodded and reached out to pluck one of the snowflakes from the air. The tiny crystals were cold to the touch, but refused to melt.

"They look like glass!" he said, and held the tiny ornament to his eye.

"They certainly do! You know they taste like sweet vanilla when they're like this?" Santa said.

"Vanilla? Why?"

"I have never been able to solve that particular riddle," Santa replied. "All I know is that when I slow time, they practically stop melting, and they taste like...well...they taste like sweet vanilla candy! Try one."

Jimmy began to laugh and placed the snowflake on his tongue. To his surprise it tasted exactly like vanilla, a sweet, candy-like flavor!

"Wow!"

"I like to add them to my cocoa as I fly," Santa said. "They don't melt straight away and they don't chill the cocoa, but they do add a nice spice! They are strange little gifts when they're like this!"

Jimmy rolled the snowflake around on his tongue and smiled.

"Watch this!" Santa said, and scooped a handful of the flakes from the air. He worked them for a moment and molded a small Christmas tree out of the crystals. He finished his sculpture by giving it a tiny blow. The snowflake tree twisted and sparkled in his hand for a moment, and Santa left it spinning in midair. "Pretty, isn't it?"

15

Jimmy clapped.

"Well, let's go, then! We have quite a distance to cover tonight!" Santa said, and continued to trudge through the pristine snow. In his wake he left a great round tunnel through the suspended flakes.

A moment later the two stepped around a large brick chimney, and there stood Santa's sleigh behind eight magnificent reindeer. Jimmy gasped at the wonderful sight. Each reindeer turned, looked from Santa to Jimmy, and bowed their heads low.

CHAPTER 5

OLD FRIENDS

"Do you think you can remember all of their names?" Santa asked.

Jimmy cleared his throat, let out a small 'hmm,' and turned his attention to the front of the line. He then pointed at one reindeer after the next, "Dasher, Dancer, Prancer, Vixen, Comet, Cupid, Donner, and Blitzen."

The reindeer stomped their hooves in approval, and Jimmy was sure they each smiled.

Santa grinned. "That's right!" He turned to his team. "I told you lot he wouldn't forget!"

"I think...I think I sorta remember a little bit about that Christmas Eve, now," Jimmy said. "At least a little bit?"

"Starting to come back, is it?" Santa asked. "Well, why don't we see if we can jog a few more of those memories free? Take the reins!"

Jimmy's breath caught in his chest as Santa motioned for him to mount the giant sleigh first. "The reins? You mean drive?"

"Well, why not? You've driven it before!"

"I have?"

Santa laughed again. "Hop on up and let's see what happens."

Jimmy climbed up and into the sleigh, scooting over so Santa could board. The interior of the sled was lined with deep red velvet and pure white cotton. It was cozy, warm, and smelled of spiced apples and oranges.

"So take these...." Santa said, and handed Jimmy the leads. Each was a colorful display of woven thread which gave off a small amount of heat and glimmered as if some sort of malleable metal had been woven into the strands. "Just give 'em a soft tug and ask Dasher to take us to the elves."

"Are you sure?" Jimmy asked. "I mean, I don't remember ever driving your sleigh."

Santa chuckled. "Of course! Take us out, Master Jim."

Jimmy laughed a sort of nervous laugh and gave the colorful reigns a small tug. "To the elves, if you please!" he asked, his voice a bit low and a tad nervous.

Nothing happened.

Santa leaned over and whispered. "A little louder... Sound like you really mean it!"

Jimmy cleared his throat and was surprised no painful coughs or jarring rattles followed. "To the elves, if you please!" he said with a bit more volume.

Dasher's ears perked. He reared, and the rest of the line charged forward. The sleigh bolted and, in an instant, launched from the roof out over the small woodland surrounding St. Joseph's hospital.

Jimmy was thrown back into the padded seat and pinned there. "WOW!!!" he shouted through a grin and above the sudden surge of wind.

Santa laughed. "That's more like it! See how the sleigh cuts through the snow?"

Jimmy glanced over his shoulder, and there behind them, suspended mid-air, was a pearly white tunnel.

Santa pointed to Dasher. "Notice the small bits of light glittering and trailing off of his antlers now?"

Jimmy nodded as he watched what appeared to a shower of glimmering glitter trail behind Dasher's wonderful antlers.

Santa smiled. "I'm not certain how they do that, but the light seems to push aside the wind and snow just as easily as the dark!"

"Has he always had antlers like that?"

"Oh yes. I'm not sure even Elvin magic could create something that wonderful. That, Master Jim, is Mother Nature's work!"

"Do any of the other reindeer's antlers glow?"

"Not that I've seen. Even the elves say they've never known another reindeer to possess such a gift, and some of them have been around quite a bit longer than me! I do know of several reindeer very different from the rest, some with coats of the purest white. Not only is their fur white, but so are their antlers, even their hooves! And each one of them have icy baby-blue eyes. There are a few solid black reindeer who call the North Pole home as well. They have the darkest fur I've ever seen; when you look at it close enough, it seems almost dark blue, perhaps deep purple in places. Beautiful creatures they are. But none, to the best of my knowledge, have antlers like Dasher's."

"I guess that makes him pretty special."

"Special, indeed!" Santa agreed.

The team charged out over the trees and began to circle around a tight gathering of pines.

"Dasher will take it from here," Santa said.

Just then, the reindeer plunged towards the earth, guiding the sleigh between the branches without so much as a bounce or a bump. When they touched ground, a small hiss rose from the runners as they raced across the snow and ice. Dasher pranced through the forest, threading the team between trees and snow-covered brush. Ahead, a soft green and amber light pulsed, casting strange whimsical shadows all about. Dasher made his way straight towards it.

"Is that them?" Jimmy asked.

"Those are the elves all right," Santa said. "Smell the cooking?"

Jimmy sniffed the air and was about to tell Santa all he could smell were the pine trees, when there, hidden just behind the forest's aromas, the scent of hot fruit and fresh bread began to grow.

"I think…I think I do!"

"Leave elves to their own devices for very long, and you're bound to be treated to some of the best baking you have ever had!" Santa said. "Which helps explain my expanding shadow!"

Jimmy laughed.

The trees gave way to a large round clearing. In the center, an enormous golden fire roared bright. Gathered around the warm blaze were fifty to sixty tiny elves, all busy with minuscule pots, pans, and stone ovens.

CHAPTER 6

ELVIN ENTRÉES

"It's Santa! He has Master Jimmy, he does!" one of the little elves cried out.

"I told you he would want to come!" Santa replied, and waved.

At the sight of the sleigh, all of the elves stopped what they were doing and ran to greet the team and passengers. Several cheers of "Hip-Hip-Hooray!" erupted from the gathering.

Jimmy watched a small ocean of striped caps bob around the team. Some were green and white, some red and white, while others were gold or silver and white.

Santa motioned to the growing crowd. "Notice the caps? The stripes, particularly the white ones, those represent the snow which surrounds our homes year-round," he said. "Actually, quite a few of the elves build their dwellings with the snow and ice, so I guess it quite literally surrounds them!"

Jimmy smiled.

"Master Jimmy! It's Krikin! Remember me?" one of the elves called out above the chattering below.

Jimmy looked over and spotted a round, smiling face with green eyes blinking up at him. A faded memory of the elf came charging back into focus, and Jimmy recalled decorating presents with him several years before. The two had sat in his parents' living room and wrapped presents for his parents while Santa ate another of his mother's cookies.

"Hello, Krikin!" Jimmy called back, and waved.

"He remembers me!!!" The elf beamed, stumbled backwards in his enthusiasm, and vanished amongst the boisterous bunch.

Santa stood when the sleigh came to a stop and raised his hands. "All right then, my friends! Let's allow the young man some food and drink before we badger him too terribly much. It's a long flight, you know!"

Another cheer erupted from the crowd, and the elves dispersed at once to their stoves, tables, pots, pans, and baskets.

"Music!" one of the elves cried out.

As Jimmy and Santa climbed down, Tchaikovsky's *Nutcracker Suite* began to drift through the cold night air from a source unseen.

"Oh, they love this one," Santa said upon hearing the melody. "If I had to choose, I would say that this is my favorite by Master Tchaikovsky."

"It's pretty."

"One of the prettiest. You know he caught me one year, too, now that I think about it," Santa said. He began to chuckle as he recalled the encounter. "I believe he was maybe six years old when he snuck up on me? Not only did he demand to know who I was, but he insisted on speaking with me in French! I thought this was strange coming from such a young and clearly Russian little boy. I had no idea why he wished to use the language, but young Pyotr was adamant about it; truly adamant. Not until now, all of these years later, when I listen to his compositions, do I understand why.

Both the French language and his marvelous music are such lovely melodic sounds. I believe he was hearing the similarities in his mind, even at such an early age."

Santa finished his little tale and led Jimmy through the crowd to a pair of nice, well-padded chairs by the giant bonfire. Each seat was a dark ruby red with gold embroidery, wooden legs, and matching fleece blanket. Jimmy plopped into his, covered his legs, and smiled as the chair began to warm him.

"Did you bring all of this with you?" Jimmy asked, motioning to the various pieces of furniture and cooking appliances.

"Oh, no—" Santa started, but was interrupted as a small, red-haired elf handed him a steaming cup of peppermint cocoa, complete with candy cane. "Thank you kindly, Burgundy," he said to the elf, and looked back at Jimmy. "No, the elves conjured all of this on their own. Never ones to be far from a good fire and cooking supplies!"

Burgundy returned a moment later and handed Jimmy his own cup of cocoa. Jimmy thanked the grinning elf and chuckled as Burgundy bowed and scampered back into the throng, his red hair glowing in the amber firelight. The two sat there for a while sipping their drinks and watching the magical flames. Krikin reappeared and placed a small round table between the two, bowed, smiled, and clapped his hands as he skipped off to gather treats.

"The fire isn't melting the snow?" Jimmy asked as he stared at the multitude of suspended snowflakes in the air around, above, and even within the flames.

"Elvin fire," Santa replied. "Great for cooking, warming, and looking at! Horrible for drying your clothes, I'm afraid."

Burgundy and Krikin re-emerged from the sea of elves and placed two gold plates of fresh bread and caramel peaches on the small table. They produced two sets of silverware from their pockets, laid them by each setting, and raced off again.

"Oh, they made the peaches!" Santa said. "You must try them; they are astounding."

Jimmy grabbed his fork and skewered one of the steaming, caramel-covered peach slices. When it touched his tongue, an explosion of cinnamon, ginger, and vanilla filled his mouth. Right behind those amazing flavors the pungent peach burst forth.

"Wow! Vewy goowd!" he said through a mouthful of forgotten manners.

Santa roared with laughter and nodded. "Yes! Yes, they are!"

For the next hour, elf after elf brought the two everything from salt-encrusted pretzels to tiny soufflés. There were cookies, cakes, and caramelized carrots to be had. Pies of all sorts were baked, sliced, and served. There were blueberry pies, apple pies, coconut pies, and even strawberry rhubarb pies. But Jimmy's favorites were the many flavors of fudge. Chocolate, vanilla, rum raisin, orange-vanilla, and peanut butter were just a few of the flavors he was offered. The best part was that Jimmy never felt full. He could eat as much as he desired and sample everything he was offered. Nothing went to waste.

The elves sang, danced, and indulged in treats. Some built snowmen, some decorated the trees, and some conjured wonderfully colored fireworks which would swoosh, swish, and hiss into the air, where they popped into brilliant illuminated life. On occasion an elf would stop by, introduce him or herself to Jimmy, and return to the merrymaking. The longer Jimmy watched, the more he remembered of the elves.

There was Krikin, Burgundy, Nobble, Tripp, Pimsy, Crissy, Jade, and even a Max among the bunch. Dasher seemed especially fond of a blonde-haired elf with a blue cap and coat who made his way around the reindeer, stopping here and there to check their teeth and then move on. The two seemed like old friends.

After a time, Santa stood and clapped his hands, took off his hat, and bowed to the elves. "Brilliant as usual, my friends! Thank you all very, very much! Your new blueberry and orange cookies were stupendous!"

Jubilant cheers erupted everywhere.

Jimmy stood and thanked the elves as well and was answered by more merry applause and lively whistles.

"Now, shall we be on our way?" Santa asked.

There was a final eruption of cheerful shouts and flashes of emerald green light began to sparkle and wink all about the camp. The fire was squelched, each tiny stove vanished, and the woodland clearing soon looked as pristine as the new snow had intended it to be. Even the thousands of tiny footprints disappeared.

"I wish I was that good at cleaning my workshop," Santa said.

Jimmy laughed. "I'll bet my mom wishes I was that good at cleaning my room!"

This brought a good chuckle from Santa, but a sudden, stinging heartache filled Jimmy's chest. He couldn't remember the last time he'd been at home, or slept in his own bed, much less cleaned his bedroom. Jimmy was fighting to swallow a harsh lump in his throat when a soft hand patted his shoulder. He looked up to see Santa smiling down at him. The weight on Jimmy's heart lifted, and he pushed the sad thought from his mind.

The two continued to watch as the multitude began to file towards the sleigh. One by one, the elves clamored up onto the sled and scampered into a giant crimson velvet bag in the rear compartment.

"We will have to join them for a while once we're off," Santa said when he noticed Jimmy's shocked expression.

"In there?" Jimmy asked, and pointed to the bag.

Santa laughed. "One of the best ways to travel if you ask me! A gift from Mrs. Claus. And don't worry, we'll all fit."

25

Jimmy blinked and grinned. "Okay?"

The last elf hopped into the sleigh and wiggled into the bag. Santa climbed on next and took the reins. As Jimmy boarded, he heard new festive music and laughter from inside the giant red sack, but his attention was soon directed towards the reindeer as they began speeding forward through the trees.

CHAPTER 7

NORTHWARD BOUND!

S anta called to the reindeer as they sped through the forest and let out a boisterous "Woo-hoo!" when Dasher leapt into the air. The team launched upward into the frozen storm with such speed that Jimmy couldn't help but laugh and cheer with excitement.

Jimmy peered over the side of the sleigh at the treetops which raced by just inches below. The light from Dasher's antlers cast a warm glow over them and flashed off of the snow covered floor beyond.

"I always love that part!" Santa said as they climbed higher and higher.

The icy forest fell away and vanished below the snow-burdened clouds. There was a brief moment when all Jimmy could see was dark gray mist, but then the team burst through the storm and into crisp, clear night air. The stars glimmered as bright as Jimmy had ever seen, and the silver moon was even more brilliant.

"They look like silver waves, don't they?" Santa said, pointing down to the ocean of clouds below.

Jimmy hung his head over the side of the sleigh and marveled. "They do! They look like silver cotton candy!"

Santa glanced back down at the clouds and began to laugh. "I've never thought of them like that, but I'd have to agree! I wonder if the elves could figure that out. Remind me to ask them sometime; silver cotton candy indeed. You should see the clouds in July just before dusk or right before dawn! Then they really look like cotton candy!"

"I would like to see that someday," Jimmy replied.

Santa looked over and patted Jimmy on the shoulder again. "Perhaps you will, Jim; perhaps you will."

The two sat in silence for a while as Dasher led the team north. Jimmy gazed about as wonderful seas of clouds rolled by, sometimes crashing against the sides of the colossal mountains which broke their surfaces here and there. Santa poured them both more hot cocoa and produced a small silver tray of warm sugar cookies. The night air was frigid, but the sleigh seemed to warm itself every now and then. Jimmy's new coat and boots did a wonderful job at combating the chilly wind whenever it crept in. As the moon vanished over the horizon, the night fell deeper into shadow, and Dasher's antlers began to glow even brighter. As the darkness increased, hundreds of tiny candles sprung to life around the sleigh's frame.

"Those are pretty," Jimmy said when the candles materialized.

"You like them?" Santa asked. "Elvin fire again. I've traveled about as fast as the reindeer dare go and I've never seen a single one of their flames so much as flicker in the wind. They help keep the cabin cozy and bright as we fly too! Speaking of which, are you warm enough?"

Jimmy nodded.

"Good, good! This new sleigh sure is a bit warmer than the first one!"

"Did the elves build it?" Jimmy asked.

"Oh, the elves and I worked on this one for the better part of a year. They are masters of most crafts, but they are exceptionally gifted when it comes to designing sleighs. The seats warm themselves; the candles appear when it gets too dark; even the reins are warm to the touch when they need be."

"I wish my parents' car had heated seats! I have to crawl under a blanket in the winter whenever we drive anywhere."

Santa laughed. "Well, don't you worry; I'm currently working with a few children on that. Hopefully when they are grown, a few of them will remember our designs."

Jimmy grinned. "You know, my grandpa told me that he met you once."

"Young James? Oh, he most certainly did! In fact, I met all of your grandparents at one time or another, both on your father's side of the family as well as your mother's. They were wonderful people."

Jimmy nodded. "I wish I had known them longer."

"Well Jim, it's not the amount of time you spend with those you love, it's the quality of the time spent. But I must confess...I miss them quite a bit as well."

"Grandpa James said you were dressed in green when he met you, green and blue. Do you not always wear the red outfit?"

"Oh no, but I do believe it's my favorite. The elves and Mrs. Claus have made me many fine garments over the years. I have everything from white and gold to purple and orange! But the red just does something for me. Ah yes, speaking of the elves, would you like to visit with them for a while as we fly?" Santa asked.

Jimmy looked over his shoulder and into the red velvet bag. All he could see were dark shadows beyond the opening.

"We'll fit?" he asked.

Santa grinned and winked. "If I can fit, anyone can!"

Jimmy laughed and watched as Santa tied the reins to a small silver bell on the sleigh's frame. "All right, Dasher! Young Master

Jim and I are going to retire for a time. You know the way! Straight and true, if you please!"

From the front of the team, Dasher turned his head and nodded.

"Shall we?" Santa asked.

Jimmy agreed, and Santa held open the bag. A warm gust of air, followed by the sounds of music and laughter, filled the sleigh. Right behind them, the strong scent of even more treats and candies being made rushed from the strange sack.

"After you!" Santa said.

Jimmy grinned and climbed over the back of the sleigh and into the rucksack. As he crawled along, he found himself navigating a rather lengthy and soft velvet tunnel. The air grew warmer and the sounds of the wind outside faded behind him the further along he crept. After a short time, almost all of the candlelight pouring into the mysterious sack behind him faded away, and Jimmy moved forward in almost complete darkness. It was a strange sensation of impractical physics: Jimmy knew he must have crawled at least the distance of one of the long hallways back at the ward, but that was impossible—wasn't it? Though come to think of it, everything about tonight was impossible. He guessed that that's just how magic is sometimes! Quite impossible and very possible all at the same wonderful time.

Just as Jimmy was wondering how much further he had to go, a mellow amber light appeared in the distance. He continued on and soon found himself looking down upon an enormous room some fifty to even seventy feet below. Just in front of him, a polished wooden slide stretched down to the floor and emptied out onto what looked like the exact same chair he'd used back in the forest. Jimmy inched himself out, pushed off, and raced towards the great room below. A few hurried seconds later, he landed in his chair with a plop and a delighted laugh. His seat slid to the right, and out popped Santa into his own matching chair.

Santa looked over at Jimmy and stood. "I told you we'd fit!" he said. He then turned to the room before them and motioned. "Welcome to the best travel lodge this side of the equator! Get it? Travel lodge?" he asked, and winked. "It's a lodge that travels!"

Jimmy laughed.

The hall was enormous. It easily dwarfed the children's ward. The new thought of the hospital sent a short-lived chill into Jimmy's stomach, but he pushed it away and continued to inspect his new surroundings. Three long wooden tables the color of dark caramel stretched the entire length of the room, and various Christmas trees lined the walls, each decorated more brilliantly than the next. Beautifully-crafted gold chandeliers hung from the ceiling, although they looked as if they'd been grown and not crafted. Giant red and green candles were fixed to each, casting a wonderful warm glow all about.

At the far end of the room stood a large wooden bar where silver steins of eggnog, cider, and various other beverages were being served. Towering behind the bar were dozens upon dozens of huge casks, each with its own ornate label carved into the front and gilded in gold, silver, or copper. The wonderful kegs had been stacked one atop the other a good fifty feet into the air. Some were even lined with bright multi-colored fairy lights, and Jimmy suspected those barrels contained the most special of spirits. There was everything from port, to wine, to strawberry ale. There were also cinnamon ciders, cocoas, and juice of every flavor imaginable.

"Would you like some eggnog?" Santa asked. "Or would you like to try one of the sodas? Perhaps a chocolate-blueberry!"

Jimmy tore his gaze from the festive room and looked up at Santa. "Chocolate and blueberry pop?"

Santa began to laugh. "It's quite good! Shall we?" he asked, and began threading his way through the tables and elves.

Jimmy followed and found himself humming along to the various holiday tunes drifting in the air like some magical breeze.

31

The two reached the bar and were greeted again by Krikin, who now sported a long brown apron adorned with dozens of tiny silver bells which jingled when he moved.

"Greetings!" the elf said.

"Hello again, Krikin," Santa replied. "We'll have two chocolate-blueberry soda pops, if you please."

Krikin nodded and grinned. "It's especially good this year, Santa! The bears sure do know how to grow those blueberries!" he said, skipping off to a tall ladder leading up to one of the topmost barrels. Krikin aimed the ladder at a brilliant indigo-stained keg with blue and purple fairy lights twinkling all around its face.

"Yes, they do," Santa agreed.

A puzzled look crossed Jimmy's face. "Bears?"

"Oh, yes. There are no better berry growers in the world if you ask me! They have a nose for it, you know. Master Huck is our lead berry grower. He and Miss Olivia raise the most delicious fruits you've ever had the pleasure to taste! Their bear friends are masters at cultivating and harvesting berries of all types."

Krikin scaled the ladder as Jimmy marveled at how high the little elf climbed with such speed and grace. Krikin then reached into one of his pockets and produced a shining silver tap, which he pressed through the wood with ease. He twisted the device several times and pulled two steins from behind his apron, which he filled with a dark blue, frothy liquid. When both steins were full, Krikin held each in a single hand, closed off his tap, and in one well-balanced maneuver, slid down the ladder back to the bar. He never spilled a drop.

"Here you are! Two chocolate-blueberry sodas! Would you like those with or without vanilla ice cream?" Krikin asked.

Santa looked to Jimmy.

"With, please," Jimmy replied.

"And I will have the same," Santa added.

Krikin reached back behind his apron and produced an already full ice cream scoop. He dropped a round ball of the treat into each drink with a plop and fizz, returned the scoop to whatever secret hiding spot from whence it had come, and placed long straws and spoons into each soda.

"Enjoy!" Krikin said, and raced off to fill another order further down the bar.

"After you," Santa said.

Jimmy pulled his stein closer and took a long sip from the straw. The soda tasted just as he thought it would. Bubbly, choco-late-y, blueberry-y and vanilla-y!

"That's really, really good!" Jimmy said.

Santa smiled and sipped his own soda, careful not to get any on his beard.

Krikin reappeared a second later. "I almost forgot!" he said. "We have some new straws this year! Cinnamon curly-Q's, they're calling 'em! Try the soda through these!"

Krikin placed the two new straws into each stein and sped away again. Santa and Jimmy marveled over the two curly straws and sipped their drinks through the new utensils.

"That's even better!" Jimmy said.

Santa was too busy nodding in agreement and sucking his straw to reply, but he winked in approval.

CHAPTER 8

ELF SCHOOL

When Santa and Jimmy finished their sodas, Krikin reappeared, took their empty steins, and wiped the counter clean.

"Thank you so much, Krikin! If you will excuse me for a while, I'd like to check in on the team," Santa said, then looked at Jimmy. "I think Krikin wanted to show you a few things as well."

At the mention of his name, Krikin beamed. "Would you like to learn a little baking magic, Master Jim?"

"Yes, please!"

"I will leave you to it," Santa said. "Save me some of whatever it is you decide to create!"

"Oh, we will, Santa!" Krikin replied.

"Splendid," Santa said, and strolled away towards the rear of the lodge.

"And for you!" Krikin said, as he produced another apron from behind his own. "Your first tool!"

Jimmy took the apron and pulled the top straps over his head. It looked very much like Krikin's, although the bells were gold and red, not silver. "Thank you!" he said as he'd tied the apron behind him.

"My pleasure!" Krikin replied. "You'll graduate to silver bells soon enough if I have anything to say about it."

"I was going to ask you if the different colors meant something," Jimmy said.

"Well, there's gold and red, like yours. That's for beginners. Then there's gold, red and green. That's for intermediate. And then there's gold, red, green and blue. That's for advanced. And finally, when you're ready, there's silver!"

"Wow!" Jimmy said. "How long did it take you to get silver?"

Krikin paused for a moment, seemed on the verge of replying, hesitated, cocked his head, started to answer, stopped, and finally clapped his hands. "Two hundred and three... no four years, seven months, five days, eleven hours, eight minutes and twenty-two, no... twenty-three seconds!"

"Ummm..." Jimmy replied.

"Yeah, I kept forgetting a few tricks," Krikin said, and shrugged. "But I got 'em! Burgundy's on year number three hundred and eleven, but I think he'll get it any day now!"

"Three hundred and...wow...."

"Wow is right! It's a lot of fun. Has to be if you're going to spend that much time learning something, right?"

Jimmy chuckled. "I guess so!"

"And you guess right! So meet me at the end of the bar, and we'll get started!"

Krikin raced away, and Jimmy followed. As he walked, each elf smiled and greeted him as he passed. By the time he reached the end of the bar, Krikin was holding a medium-sized glass bowl, which in turn held a silver whisk, two dark wooden spoons, and a bag of something Jimmy could not make out.

"Here you go!" Krikin said. "Your second, third, fourth and fifth tools!" he added, and handed over the bowl and its contents.

DAVID S. SHOCKLEY II

"Thank you!"

"Are you teaching Master Jim to cook?" a pretty-sounding voice asked from far down one of the long tables.

Jimmy turned and spotted a small blonde-haired elf smiling back at them.

"Would you like to help?" Krikin asked.

"Would I?" the elf replied. She clapped her hands, stood, and hurried down the table. "Would I ever! Hello!" she said, and shook Jimmy's hand with enthusiastic vigor.

"Hello!" Jimmy replied.

"My name is Primrose!" the little elf said, and pointed to her blonde hair. Strewn about her curly locks were beautiful pale yellow flowers which seemed to glow. "These are my favorite flowers ever! So the name stuck! Primrose! But you can call me Pimsy. Or Pim, or maybe Pim-Pim, or even Pimpermint if you like," she said, and began to giggle.

"I like Pimsy! That's a fun name," Jimmy said. He motioned to the little flowers nestled in the elf's hair. "And those are really pretty!"

"She's fun, all right!" Krikin added.

"Why, thank you, Master Jim!" Pimsy blushed and winked at Krikin as she pulled an apron from her pocket.

As she tied her apron tight, Jimmy noticed Pimsy's bells were gold and red, just like his. "I guess we're both beginners!"

Pimsy glanced down at her apron and giggled. "Yes, we are! I've only been at it for a little while. No more than twenty, thirty years."

Krikin cocked his head.

"Maybe forty," Pimsy said, and began to chuckle even more.

Jimmy's eyes widened. "Wow."

"Let's just try a simple batch of gingerbread people!" Krikin suggested. "Would you like to use gumdrops? Or icing? Or both?"

"How about both?" Jimmy replied.

"Yes, both!" Pimsy agreed.

Krikin was about to speak when another voice called out over the chatter and singing. "Krikin! Are you holding a baking lesson?"

"I'd like to!" Krikin called back. "If I can ever—"

"Baking classes?" another voice shouted.

"...get started." Krikin finished.

In an instant, the entire lodge began to gather around Krikin, Jimmy, and Pimsy. Each elf pulled an apron over their head and waited eagerly for Krikin's instructions. Jimmy noted that not all of the elves were beginners, and more than a handful had aprons with all silver bells.

Krikin cleared his throat. "Well, if everyone's ready, I think we should start with a simple song, yes?"

There was a murmur of agreement, and Krikin bounded onto the nearest tabletop. "If you would, Master Jimmy!" he said, and held out his hand.

Jimmy took Krikin's lead and stepped up onto the table alongside the elf. There was a loud cheer, and Krikin produced his own bowl complete with spoons, whisk, and an identical bag.

"It's rather simple, actually," Krikin began. "All you have to do is sing along as best you can! Listen to the chorus, and sing that once you've picked it up! When you think you've remembered the rest, just join in!"

"That's it?" Jimmy said. "All I have to do is sing?"

A small wave of kind chuckles swept through the lodge.

"Well, that and be mindful of your bowl!" Krikin replied. "And remember, baking is a lot like falling in love. You start slow, measure some carefully considered ingredients, pay close attention, add a little heat, and reap the rewards!"

"Wow, I never really thought of it like that," Jimmy replied.

Krikin smiled. "And what better way to show your love than to sing? We could all learn a thing or two from our feathered friends in the skies, am I right?"

All of the elves nodded and several "hear, hears" echoed throughout the hall.

"So let us begin!" Krikin said. The elves erupted into song:

Come ginger, come spice!
Come sweet and come nice!

Bring nutmeg and clove! Bring fire and stove!

Come sugar, come love!
Come spoon and come glove!

Bring nutmeg and clove! Bring fire and stove!

Come honey, come rum!
Come grape and come plum!

Bring nutmeg and clove! Bring fire and stove!

Come gumdrops, come creams!
Come laughs and come dreams!

Bring nutmeg and clove! Bring fire and stove!

It wasn't long before Jimmy could sing the chorus, and shortly thereafter he was able to sing the entire song without fail. As soon as he began, his bowl and its contents sprang to life! Jimmy stepped back at once and watched as his utensils floated out over the table and began twisting and twirling about. He never once stopped singing. The air above the table was soon thick with dancing tools and crockery.

"Now don't stop the song!" Krikin said as Jimmy began to giggle.

Jimmy sang on and watched his bowl perform. The spoons and whisk twirled about one another as the small bag opened and upturned its contents into the glass bowl. There was a small shower of golden sparks and out of nowhere, bottles of cold milk began to visit one dish after the other. These were followed by hundreds of cream-colored eggs which cracked themselves, spilled their bright orange contents into the mixtures, and disappeared, leaving no mess whatsoever. The spoons and whisks began their jobs after that, mixing and kneading the pungent dough this way and that.

"Here's the fun part!" Krikin said between verses.

Just then, all of the bowls, spoons, and whisks raced off to the far end of the lodge and disappeared behind the bar. Behind them, they left suspended in midair perfectly round balls of Gingerbread Cookie dough.

"Where did they go?" Jimmy asked.

Krikin finished the chorus he'd begun and chuckled. "They've gone to wash and dry themselves so we can continue!"

The elves stopped their song and the balls of dough floated down in front of each.

"Well done, everyone! Well done, indeed!" Krikin said, and clapped his hands loudly.

Jimmy poked his floating ball of dough gingerly. It wavered in the air and spun a sort of lazy spiral.

"And we only had one mishap!" one of the elves called out and pointed.

There at the end of the table stood Burgundy, his hat, coat, and apron covered in flour and eggs. Despite the mess that caked his clothing and face, Burgundy was laughing hysterically.

"I...." he began and started laughing again. "I...I sang the wrong song! And then..." Burgundy chuckled harder, tears cleaning bright pink streaks down his flour-caked cheeks. "And then I...I forgot the lyrics for gingerbread dough!"

An eruption of snickers filled the hall, and several elves began helping poor Burgundy clean himself. They too were laughing hard.

"I started singing the song for ice cream!" Burgundy gasped. "And the eggs! The eggs came from all directions!" Burgundy said and fell over, lost in contagious hysterics.

"Well, at least it wasn't me this time!" Pimsy said.

Krikin chuckled and patted the blonde elf on the back.

CHAPTER 9

BAKING WITH LOVE AND CARE

The next song was even easier for Jimmy to remember. The sections he liked best were for frosting and making up his own lyrics for whichever colors he wished to use. Krikin helped a little by warning Jimmy not to try for orange, as even the silver-belled cooks were still attempting to rhyme that one.

The rolling pin song was a rollicking, rambunctious one, and the cookie cutter song was quick, sharp, and precise. When the air was saturated with dancing gingerbread people, tiny silver ovens appeared on the walls all about the lodge. They stretched from floor to ceiling and were instantly hard at hot work. Jimmy marveled as the unbaked cookies formed long dancing lines towards the ovens. They each took turns lying down on golden cookie sheets, baking, and then re-emerging to dance away for their chance to be decorated.

It wasn't long before thousands of gumdrops, millions of candies, and hundreds of frosting-covered brushes raced through the pungent, spice-laden air, clothing each cookie in vibrant colors and splendid details.

"You have to love this part!" Krikin said as the cookies were decorated.

"It's wonderful!" Jimmy replied.

There were no further mishaps. Even Burgundy managed to get all of his cookies rolled, cut, baked, and frosted without further incident.

"I wish I could cook like this back home," Jimmy said.

Krikin looked unsure of what to say for a moment, and his smile faded just a bit. "Well, maybe we can help with that?" he finally said, and clapped Jimmy on the shoulder.

A shadow fell across Pimsy's smile for a moment as well as she glanced from Krikin to Jimmy and then to her little feet. Before Jimmy could comment on the elves' strange behavior, Pimsy sparked up.

"Try one of my cookies! I added cherry and lemon to the batter this time!"

Jimmy accepted one of the cookies and took a bite. It was delicious.

"And eggnog! What say you all? To the bar?" Krikin shouted.

A loud cheer rose up from the elves, and everyone began working their way across the lodge. The gingerbread cookies followed and stacked themselves onto plates which had appeared at various locations.

"And as for you, Master Jim," Krikin said, "you've more than earned this!"

Krikin pulled a tiny gold pin from his pocket and fastened it to Jimmy's apron. The pin was a tiny Gingerbread cookie and sparkled brilliantly as the light danced across its surface.

"Your cookies were top-notch if I don't say so myself!"

"Thank you, Krikin," Jimmy said.

"No, Master Jim, thank you!" replied the elf, and took a huge bite from one of Jimmy's cookies. The colorful green and red frosting stained the little elf's lips until he licked them clean with a silly smile and a cheerful chuckle. "Thank you very much!"

Jimmy laughed. "You're welcome!"

Santa returned about an hour later. He popped out of the hole in the wall and landed in one of the plush chairs below, all chuckles and smiles. He inspected Jimmy's first go at Elvin baking and was very impressed, so much so that he tucked a few of Jimmy's gingerbread men into his pocket for later. Krikin seemed pleased that Santa was happy and beamed for the next several hours.

Santa and Jimmy retired to a pair of large, plush chairs in front of a warm cozy fire flanked by two stunning Christmas trees. The trees were adorned with more decorations and more lights than Jimmy had ever seen on a single Christmas tree. They took your breath away when you saw them and pulled your gaze ever deeper and deeper into the brilliantly decorated branches.

"Dasher tells me we'll be home very soon!" Santa said. "Would you like to see everything from the air as we arrive?"

"That would be great!" Jimmy replied.

"Well, we should head up soon, then,"

Jimmy nodded and looked back towards the crowded bar. Krikin was busy pouring more drinks and stopping whenever he could to chat with little Pimsy.

"Santa… can I ask you a question?"

"But of course."

"Well…" Jimmy paused for a moment, then cleared his throat. "Well, earlier, just for a minute, Krikin and Pimsy looked worried when I mentioned my home. And… well, I'm not sure why?"

Santa sat quiet for a moment, and then retrieved a long white pipe from his pocket. He lit the end with a tiny wooden match and blew a smoke ring into the fire, where it floated up the chimney and disappeared.

43

"That's because Krikin and Pimsy are worried about you, Jim," he replied.

"Because I've been so sick?"

Santa nodded. "They don't like to see anyone hurt or ill. And they know all too well how badly you've felt over the last few months."

Jimmy looked back to the flames and sighed. "I don't think my parents are telling me the truth about it."

Santa looked over and stared at Jimmy, his eyes narrowed. "That's because they love you very, very much, Jim. So much, in fact, that they refuse to believe what you already know."

Jimmy was silent for a time and stared at the fire before them. "I'm not going to get better, am I?" he asked after a bit. Several tears spilled out over his cheeks.

Santa patted Jimmy on the knee and winked. "You let me worry about that, Jim. Ol' Santa has more up his sleeves than cookies!"

Jimmy wanted to believe the jolly old elf. He wished he could forget about the hospital, about the pains in his chest, the coughing fits which woke him in the dark of night, and the horrible medicines he had to endure. He wanted more than anything to forget these things, but somewhere, someplace deep in his heart, he knew he couldn't. Jimmy forced a smile, which felt about as real as the hope he had of getting better, and nodded to Santa.

Santa smiled and patted Jimmy's knee again. "Why don't we head up and watch Dasher bring us in for a landing?"

The thought of returning to the cold winter air frightened Jimmy for a moment, and he felt a small cough struggle to life far down in his chest. He shook off the feeling and forced himself to remember that Santa's sleigh was as warm as a bright summer's day, and stood to go.

Santa smiled. "Splendid."

CHAPTER 10

THE NORTH POLE

The trip out of Santa's magical bag was not what Jimmy expected at all. When they reached the rear of the lodge, Jimmy spotted the hole from which he and Santa had climbed, noting how much higher it seemed. The opening, now framed in beautiful dark wood, rested a good sixty to sixty-five feet up the brick wall. How they would reach it mystified Jimmy—until Santa provided a wondrous solution. He simply whistled three times, and a glass staircase shimmered into existence before them. Again, Jimmy's jaw dropped, and he found it impossible not to stare at his feet as they climbed, thinking that at any moment the glass would give way and they'd tumble to the floor far below. The glass staircase looked so thin and delicate that the fact it was holding its own weight was astonishing, and witnessing it hold his and Santa's combined weight was almost unbelievable. Of course, the staircase held just fine, though Jimmy held his breath for most of the precarious climb.

As they stepped onto the bag's red velvet, the walls expanded so Santa and Jimmy could walk side by side to the exit. No crawling was necessary this go-around. It was as if the magical sack recognized the two now and accommodated their passage. A short scramble over the seat, and both were situated comfortably back in the sleigh.

Jimmy glanced over his shoulder at the magical red bag. "Did we shrink when we climbed inside? Or did the bag grow? Or maybe we shrank while the bag grew?"

Santa chuckled. "Honestly? I think a little bit of everything. I stopped trying to understand some of the elves' magic a long time ago. Did you know most of the elves are older than me, and yet more than half of them look and act as if they are still children? It's quite a thing."

Jimmy thought about asking Santa how old he was, but considered the question rude and simply nodded.

"Older than you think," Santa said.

"What?"

"You were wondering how old I was, yes?"

"Well, yes sir, but...."

Santa laughed. "To be quite honest, I stopped counting after a while. Suffice to say, I'm older than most people think."

"Wow."

"Wow is right," Santa said, and grinned.

At the front of the team, Dasher noticed Santa and Jimmy's return and turned his head, directing the rest of the team into a steep dive towards the clouds.

"Now he's just showing off!" Santa said as he gripped the armrest.

Jimmy gasped, clutched his armrest, and began laughing as they dipped into the glowing clouds. There was a moment of gray haze, the feeling of cold mist, and the sled burst through the storm. New snow was funneled around the team, and tiny golden lights began to twinkle into view far, far below. Dasher seemed glad to be home and sped along, rising and falling in an unending rollercoaster of fantastic dips, climbs, twists, and magical, merry maneuvers.

"He thinks he's a Coney Island attraction sometimes, that boy!" Santa said, and laughed as Dasher plunged towards the earth again in the steepest dive yet.

Jimmy and Santa both cheered!

"My dad used to—" Jimmy started, but Dasher pulled the sleigh back up into the sky for another round of twists and dips, interrupting Jimmy's ability to speak for a moment. "...used to talk about the Cyclone roller coaster there," he finished when his stomach resituated itself.

"Ahh! The Cyclone! I love that coaster," Santa said. "Wait until you see the ones we've been working on here!"

"You build roller coasters?" Jimmy asked.

"Oh, we've been constructing some that won't make their debut for another forty, fifty years! Dasher loves to help the elves with their designs."

"Forty or fifty years?" Jimmy asked.

"Well, we can't start planting ideas for things in children's heads too early, you know! Sometimes we have to wait for the world's technology to catch up."

"So you can design something and teach someone how to build it without them ever knowing?"

Santa smiled. "Presents under the tree aren't the only gifts we bestow, Master Jim. The ideas for the Eiffel Tower, airplanes, and penicillin, just to name a few. That one I'm particularly proud of."

"Peni-what?"

"Cillin! It's a form of antibiotic. Meaning, it helps a lot of sick people get better. We've been working on its benefits for quite some time! It's very, very close to being used widely, so cross your fingers!"

"Could it help me?" Jimmy asked.

Santa looked over, and his smile faded a bit. "I'm afraid not, Jim. But remember, I have ideas on that, too."

Jimmy's stomach sank for a moment and Santa reached around

his shoulders and patted him gently in a warm hug. Jimmy cleared his throat and smiled.

Dasher finished a few more excited tricks and slowed the team as tiny buildings began to appear below.

Jimmy pointed. "Is that it?"

"That it is!" Santa answered.

Dasher began a soft downward spiral towards the lights. As Jimmy watched, more and more features began to take shape beyond the snow and ice. The clouds above were dark and heavy with snow, but the glow from thousands and thousands of windows lit the entire night sky regardless.

"I think we can give the snow a rest for a few moments, don't you?" Santa asked, and with a clap of his mitten-covered hands, the storm clouds above parted.

Jimmy turned his earthward gaze skyward and marveled at the array of colors that rippled and waved like giant curtains spun from rainbows.

"What is—?" Jimmy tried to ask, but lost his question amidst the waves of awe which flooded over him. He simply pointed.

"That, Master Jim, is the aurora borealis. Stunning, isn't it?"

Jimmy was still unable to speak, so he simply nodded. Out of all of the wondrous and beautiful sights he'd seen thus far, none compared to the magnificence above.

"You know, normally you can see those wonderful lights virtually every night, but I've been asking for snow on a regular basis the last few years."

"Asking for snow?"

"We're going to need it around here in the near future. At least enough to last until everyone takes care of the warming. But speaking of starting, don't get me going about all of that!"

Jimmy had no idea what Santa was talking about, but whatever it was, he seemed quite passionate on the subject.

"You'll have to forgive ol' Santa, Jim. I tend to get a little flustered over problems I can't solve quickly."

"Like the war?" Jimmy asked.

"Especially wars. You'd think one the size of the last would have been enough. But maybe you and I can do something about that? What do you say?"

Jimmy smiled. "That would be great! Maybe my dad...." He stopped as an image of his father and his uncle flashed into existence. The memory was a happy one, at a time before the war when the family was together on holiday. It was the last time Jimmy had seen Uncle Freddy. His father and Uncle looked so much alike it was hard to tell the two apart sometimes.

Santa patted Jimmy on the knee. "I know your father misses your Uncle Frederick, even more than you."

Jimmy's uncle had been killed during the first year of the war, and Jimmy's father hadn't been the same since. His letters home became less cheery, came less often, and were far, far shorter. Uncle Freddy had been a wonderful person and his father's only brother. When Jimmy and his mother received the news, they cried for days. Jimmy suspected his father cried far longer than that, even if he was a grown man. He probably still cried from time to time. Jimmy sure did.

"...and I know your father has seen more than his fair share of horrible things. But how about you and I do what we can to make some of those pains a bit easier for him?"

"Yes, thank you," Jimmy said. He turned his face and wiped away a tear or two.

"Then it's a deal! So why don't you and I put aside these woeful thoughts and enjoy ourselves?" Santa said. "It's a wonderful night after all, and you've more than just a few exciting sights to see yet!"

Jimmy nodded and smiled again as the team circled closer and closer to the ground. As they descended, buildings of all shapes came into sharper focus. There were at least two buildings that appeared to be giant lighthouses painted with red and white spirals. Atop each tower, red and green lights circled about. Dasher guided the sleigh so close to one of these towers that Jimmy spied a half-dozen elves waving at them from the highest windows. Jimmy waved back, as did Santa.

After the towers, a sprawling village came into view. Houses of wood, brick, and stone dotted the landscape. Almost every home boasted a tall brick chimney issuing forth long silver streams of smoke. The bouquet of cozy fires saturated the air. Front yards were festooned with snowmen and various ice-built structures. Millions upon millions of colored lights lined the houses, and along the streets, gas lanterns flickered and flicked, shooing away purplish shadows. Santa pointed to a line of reindeer-driven sleighs weaving their way along one of the streets. They looked very much like Santa's sled, only smaller, and giant silver carafes had been placed on the backs of two of them. Tiny streams of steam trailed off of their tops.

"Caroling and hot chocolate," Santa said as Jimmy craned his neck to get a better look. "You can't have one without the other in my opinion."

As they flew over the multitude of rooftops, the elves below cheered and waved. Eventually, the houses gave way to more complex designs. But as Jimmy looked closer, he realized that these too were homes, and each was built from ice! The cloudy silver walls were lit from fires within and pulsed with reds, greens, and blues of all shades from the colored lights strewn about.

"These are some of the oldest of the homes. You would be amazed at how warm they are, despite being built from ice!" Santa said.

"They look like magical glass."

Santa chuckled.

The ice houses soon gave way to an enormous dark green forest. Jimmy looked down and noticed many an elf below the canopy of snow encrusted emerald trees. There were frozen ponds where some skated, fires around which some sang, and long tables where some ate, drank, and sang.

"You wouldn't think giant trees and homes could be found on a sea of floating ice, would you?" Santa asked.

Jimmy shook his head. "Not unless Santa and his elves built it all!"

Santa laughed long and hard. "Well, there is that."

CHAPTER 11

A CITY BUILT FOR CHRISTMAS

T he magical forest stretched on even further than the vast village of homes had before it. At its center, the largest tree Jimmy had ever seen stood sentinel over all. The tree was more than just big, more than huge; it was an immense mountain of deep brown bark and elegant emerald leaves. Along the giant trunk and enormous branches, tiny windows carved deep into the wood pulsed with whatever fires, candles, or magic had been conjured within.

"And this, Jimmy! This is the First Tree," Santa said.

Jimmy was positive that even the aurora borealis must appreciate this grand spectacle.

"The first tree of the forest?" he asked.

"Well, in a way. But to be more precise, this is the first tree on earth. It was given to me as a gift long, long ago."

"And people live, they live inside of it?"

"Oh yes! Every year the elves take turns moving into or out of the tree. It is always a grand event to reside within its walls. Many a young elf waits anxiously for their first year there. Anxiously being a modest description at best," Santa said, and chuckled. "Why, Krikin lives there now, in fact!"

"He does?"

"Oh yes, this is his first year. I know he would be honored to give you a tour later if you would like."

"Very much so!"

"Good, good. I will arrange it, assuming I can get you out of Mrs. Claus's grip for a time."

"My mother says my grandmother used to look like Mrs. Claus. I don't really remember my grandmother all that much."

Santa smiled and looked to Jimmy. "Your mother is right. They did share an uncanny resemblance, not to mention a fondness for quilting and cooking."

Dasher made several slow passes around the First Tree, and Jimmy found it impossible to tear his eyes from it. Almost everywhere, there were windows and doors. Long wooden pathways - which appeared to have been grown instead of built - spiraled about the trees' branches. Hundred of busy elves walked to and fro. Santa called out to them by name as the sleigh glided by, and each waved while cheers floated up into cold air.

"This was also the first workshop," Santa said. "In fact, it's still the second largest shop in the north!"

"You have more than one workshop?"

Santa smiled. "Oh yes, we're up to twelve now!"

"Wow!"

"Wow, indeed. There are plans for three more in the works as we speak."

Dasher made a final pass, and the sleigh turned north again. The forest eventually gave way to more homes, only these were surrounded by large fields of emerald green, sunflower yellow, and warm shades of autumn. The snow seemed to have missed these areas entirely.

"Some of our farms," Santa said. "We grow just about every-thing you can imagine."

"The cold doesn't bother them?"

"You can't see it, but each field is covered by a magical field that keeps out the chill and snow. Do you see the glowing orbs floating about?"

Jimmy looked closer as Dasher guided the team over one of the enormous orange crops. There, bobbing about, several feet above what looked to be rows of pumpkins, three miniature suns made their way down the rows as if on patrol.

"You mean those?" he asked.

"I do! Those are elf-orbs, or elf-lights. They provide enough illumination and warmth for whatever crops the elves decide to plant. Marvelous magic, if you ask me."

"That's neat."

Santa chuckled. "Neat indeed!"

Soon what could only be described as an enormous castle appeared on the horizon. Jimmy stared as they flew closer and closer to the structure, unable to speak or close his now gaping jaw.

"Welcome to my home!" Santa said.

If the grand tree at the center of Santa's forest was the First Tree, then the castle before them was the grandparent of all castles. It appeared to encompass several diverse designs from one section to the next. White stone walls with cobalt blue roofs glistened on one side, while dark wooden structures covered another. There were square brick towers, round marble towers, stone arches, wooden arches and glass domes everywhere.

Dasher landed the sled without so much as a bump and proceeded at a canter through one of the many large entrances. The castle was obviously not built for defense, as its walls were lined with enormous windows and not a single entrance appeared to have doors or gates. High on the parapets, hundreds of elves cheered and showered the team and riders in a multitude of colored ribbons and glitter. Jimmy craned his neck so he could see the tops of the towers and walls. Lining each were cheering elves. When he looked at the buildings, the windows and doors were crowded with smiling faces. More reindeer strolled the streets, some pulling sleighs, others playing games in the snow.

The team made its way down a long row of closely huddled shops, some as tall as the towers dotting the castle walls. There was a multistory bookstore, a blacksmith, a sprawling candy store, a glass blower, a pottery maker, and a cheese shop, to name a few. As they passed a large set of stables, horses, reindeer, and even camels watched them glide by. Jimmy wasn't sure, but he thought there might have even been a polar bear or two napping in the back of one of the cozy-looking stalls.

The long street of shops opened up to a wide main boulevard which cut through the massive city from north to south. Dasher turned north towards what appeared to be Santa's house. The structure was both red brick and mahogany wood. Dozens of brightly lit windows covered every side of the home that Jimmy could see. Just in front of the house and slightly off-center stood a tall fir tree adorned with various colored lights and decorations. From each side of the street, more and more elves flooded into view to catch a glimpse of the team as they passed. Jimmy caught several of them glancing at him and smiling, then whispering something to a neighbor.

When the team stopped, Santa stood and raised a hand. A hush fell over the crowd.

"Hello, my friends!" he said.

A cheery and robust reply echoed above all.

"I've a guest, whom most of you already know. Master Jim, if you please," Santa said, and motioned for Jimmy to stand.

"Master Jim!" a voice called out.

"It is him!" a second responded.

"About time!" a third added. This was followed by laughter.

Jimmy was unsure of what to say or how, so he simply smiled and raised his hand in a timid 'hello'.

"And as I'm sure you are all aware, the hour is late, and young Jim and I are quite tired from the trip," Santa said.

"And you best not keep the missus waiting any longer, Santa!" a voice called out from the crowd. More laughter echoed about the plaza.

"No, I most certainly should not!" Santa laughed, and climbed down from the sleigh.

Jimmy followed and watched as the giant red sack in the rear of the sled floated up and out. It settled on the snow-covered ground and opened itself. Elf after elf after hopped out, and ran off to meet family and friends. Krikin appeared, followed by Pimsy, and both set about unhitching the reindeer.

"I will see you in the morning, Master Jim!" Krikin said as he guided Vixen into the crowd to do whatever it was Santa's reindeer did when not flying about.

"Thank you, Krikin!" Santa said. "Shall we go inside, Jim?"

Jimmy nodded and followed Santa up a short set of stone steps to an immense intricately carved wooden door. The giant man kicked what little snow had accumulated on the bottom of his boots free and reached for what appeared to be a crystal door knocker. He gave it three quick raps which sounded like wind-chimes in a soft breeze. Jimmy was busy removing his own shoes' snow when the door opened, and Mrs. Claus stood bathed in warm honey-colored light before them.

CHAPTER 12

MOTHER CHRISTMAS

"Hello, my dear," Santa said.

Mrs. Claus smiled and hugged her husband tight. "I was beginning to think you took Jimmy off on a tour of the workshops," she said. "And how are you, Jimmy dear? Did you have a good trip?"

Jimmy blushed. "Yes, ma'am! It was…it was…I don't know how to describe it really, but it was wonderful, I do know that!"

Mrs. Claus laughed as she hugged Jimmy long and hard. "Well, good!" she said, and ushered the two inside.

Mrs. Claus was dressed in red and white like Santa, but also wore a dark green shawl over her shoulders. Her dress was long, and a delicate white apron showed signs of recent baking. Bright silver hair wrapped in a tight bun reflected the cheery light from within the house. She hung Santa's and Jimmy's coats, hats, and mittens by the door on a long set of brightly colored glass knobs. The home was warm and smelled of cookies, spices, and strong coffee. In fact, the scent of gingerbread was so potent that Jimmy caught himself wondering if the very dwelling itself might be made of it. Anything was possible here, after all!

"Why don't you go get yourself sorted, dear, and I will see to young Jimmy," Mrs. Claus said.

"Thank you, Jessica," Santa replied, and stepped out of the room.

"Follow me, Love, and we'll get something hot in your belly to fight off the cold."

Jimmy smiled and realized that despite all he'd had to eat and drink this evening—and there had been quite a lot—the idea of having something made by Mrs. Claus herself was exhilarating. The two walked through a cozy-looking living room complete with glowing hearth and many a well-padded chair. The carpet was so lush and so soft that Jimmy caught himself wondering how wonderful it must be to curl up on it in front of the warm fire.

From there, the two strolled along a lengthy hallway lined with half a dozen doors, each painted maroon with a warm gold trim. Gas lanterns hung along the walls every few feet, their flames dancing as if waving hello. At the end of the corridor, an enormous kitchen came into view, and Jimmy noticed at least two elves busy at work. One was kneading dough, while the other hung boughs of holly.

"Jelly and Binks, meet Jimmy!" Mrs. Claus said. Startled, the two elves stopped what they were doing and looked up. They each looked quite surprised to see Jimmy and Mrs. Claus standing there, as they had been completely lost in their work.

"So...so very soon!" one of the elves said, and nearly fell from a small wooden ladder.

"Binksy! That's no way to greet our new guest," the other elf said, and skipped over to where Jimmy stood. She was smaller than most of the other elves Jimmy had seen, and her hair was a bright cobalt blue. "My name is Jelly, and this is—"

"Binks, Master Jim!" the other elf interrupted. "Well, not Binksmasterjim, but just Binks! Plain old Binks! Well, not plainoldbinks...."

"Binksy," Jelly said in a soft, calming voice. She patted her friend on the shoulder and smiled at him while pantomiming a deep, measured breath.

The flustered and clearly excited elf took a deep, slow breath. "So… so sorry…I get…I can be…Well, I get…excited sometimes!" Binks said behind now furiously blushing cheeks.

"Pleased to meet you both!" Jimmy replied.

Mrs. Claus motioned to the elves. "Why don't the two of you find Jimmy a chair, and let's see if we can show him some of what you've learned this week?"

Jelly's eyes lit up, and her hair seemed to glow for an instant. "May we?" she asked, and clapped.

"Of course, dear," Mrs. Claus replied.

Binks skipped over to Jimmy, guided the boy to a long wooden table, and began setting dishes and cutlery before him. Jimmy sat and watched as the two elves dashed about the kitchen while Mrs. Claus added more wood to the room's huge fireplace. The kitchen was the largest Jimmy had ever seen, but it still retained a, aura of comfort and coziness despite its intimidating size. The table where he now sat was festooned with baskets and ceramics containing fruits of all kinds, while half a dozen candelabras hung above, illuminating the long table with warm amber light. The candles above were all cream-colored, though their flames faded from one brilliant color to the next on occasion. Behind the enormous table, a long line of floor-to-ceiling windows looked out on a small forest of trees; the magical city glimmered just beyond.

"Jelly and Binks here are my newest students," Mrs. Claus said. "Students?"

"Oh yes, I open my doors to anyone who would like to learn a thing or two in the kitchen. The elves are wonderful cooks, if you haven't yet enjoyed that particular talent of theirs."

"Oh, yes, ma'am. Krikin and Pimsy taught me how to bake gingerbread men on the way!"

Mrs. Claus raised an eyebrow. "Did they now?"

"I have an apron in my coat by the door."

"Well, that's wonderful!" Mrs. Claus said. "Krikin was a marvelous student when he came here. Always willing to try new things and just... jump right in, so to speak!"

Jelly and Binks broke into hysterics at that. Binks actually fell to the floor, and tears began streaming down his cheeks.

"What's so funny?" Jimmy asked as he too began to chuckle.

Mrs. Claus was now snickering too. After regaining some composure, she said, "You should ask Krikin about the flour tower sometime, Jimmy. I think you will enjoy that tale."

"Flour tower?" Jimmy asked.

At the question, Jelly collapsed on top of Binks clutching her belly. "Oh stop, please!" she begged between giggles and gasps for air.

Jimmy moved the tale of Krikin and this flour tower to the top of his long list of questions and laughed despite not knowing exactly what it was he was chuckling at.

Mrs. Claus motioned about the kitchen and wiped away several giggle-tears. "When Santa and I first arrived at the North Pole, several of the elves took it upon themselves to pass along a bit of their oldest and most special of recipes. They even helped build this kitchen! In fact, it was the first room built! The rest of the house was constructed around this very room. If a home has a heart, it must be the kitchen. I've passed along what they taught me ever since."

For the next half hour, Mrs. Claus and the two elves brought Jimmy everything from hot cider to cheese soup to fresh bread. He was pleased when Santa returned and the five of them enjoyed the meal together. For dessert, there was eggnog-flavored fudge, coated in freshly ground nutmeg, infused sweet cheese, and hot butterscotch chocolate. It was divine.

"So tell me Jimmy, are you sleepy yet? And be honest, young man!" Mrs. Claus asked.

Jimmy considered the question and admitted he was beginning to grow drowsy.

"You might be the first young boy I've ever met to confess he was actually sleepy, Master Jim," Santa said, and laughed. "And I've met my fare share of children!"

Mrs. Claus patted Jimmy's arm. "You just come with me, dear. I've already made up a room for you."

"We must be going as well, missus," Binks said, and pulled a long blue coat from thin air, which he wrapped about Jelly.

"See you bright and early for breakfast!" Mrs. Claus said.

"Good night!" Jimmy said to the elves.

"Before we go, what is your favorite fruit, Master Jim?" Jelly asked, her blue hair flashing bright again.

"Umm, my favorite?"

"Yes! For your hot-cakes in the morning! I was thinking we could add some of your favorite fruit to the batter if you would like," Jelly replied. "Or maybe whip up some flavored syrup?"

Jimmy grinned. "Well, in that case, surprise me, Jelly."

The little elf's smile looked as if it would split her in two. "Oh, thank you!" Jelly said, and her hair began to glow an even brighter blue.

"It was a pleasure to meet you, Master Jim!" Binks said.

"Same to you, Binks."

"Good night, you two," Santa said, and just like that, the elves vanished in a shower of silver and gold glitter. It lingered in the air for a brilliant moment, then fell to the floor and vanished as well.

Mrs. Claus turned to Jimmy. "Now let's get you to your room."

"Pleasant dreams, Jim," Santa added, and retrieved a long white pipe from his sleeve, which he began to pack with sweet-smelling tobacco.

"Good night, Santa, and thank you!" Jimmy replied.

"Not at all Jim, not at all," Santa replied, and was soon lost in thought.

CHAPTER 13

SWEETS AND DREAMS

Mrs. Claus led Jimmy through the wonderful house to a long carpeted staircase. The handrail was wrapped in dark green holly, bright red ribbons, and shiny silver bells. On each rung hung a miniature red and white stocking, complete with embroidered name on its fluffy cuff. There were names such as Mitzer, Tawney, Veep, Vop, and even a Vippy on the tiny stockings.

"Our house guests," Mrs. Claus commented when she noticed Jimmy inspecting the tiny socks.

Jimmy was very tired now and did not think to ask who precisely the house guests were, if they, too, were visiting like him, or even how large the house was considering it was clearly accommodating a large number of simultaneous guests.

At the top of the stairs, Mrs. Claus turned left and strolled down an even longer hallway than before. It was lined with doors of different sizes. Some were no larger than the tiny elf Jelly, while some were far, far smaller. Other doors were as big as Santa himself, and several more were just the size to fit a young child like Jimmy. More than a few were stacked atop one another, with tiny staircases built into the walls for access. Jimmy noticed one of the smallest doors, maybe the size of his hand, had been decorated with a miniature green wreath complete with tiny twinkling lights which flashed emerald and crimson from time to time.

"And here we are, dear," Mrs. Claus said. She placed a gentle hand on Jimmy's shoulder and motioned to a door just taller than he.

"Now if you need anything, anything at all, you will find a small bell by the bed. Simply give it a ring, and someone will be here in a jiffy. You will also find a large bath just down the hall there, and plenty of clothes which I'm sure will fit you just fine."

"Thank you," Jimmy said.

"You are quite welcome, dear."

Mrs. Claus turned, began to hum, and strolled back down the hallway, eventually vanishing around the corner. Jimmy opened the bedroom door and stepped into his room. Before him, a great round rug covered most of a highly polished, chocolate-colored wooden floor. On his right burned a warm orange fire within a stone hearth. Before the fireplace stood a stained glass spark guard depicting a shining gold star above an emerald green forest. An enormous, comfy-looking bed sat before a multi-paned window nook. The window protruded out of the room several feet, and the nook itself was lined with maroon, blue, and green pillows. The plaza and Christmas tree below lit what little the fire did not within the bedroom. The bed itself was covered in a multitude of comforters and quilts and appeared to be the softest thing Jimmy had ever touched. He was keen to find out.

Sure enough, beside the bed stood a nightstand complete with lamp and tiny silver bell as promised. Next to the bell rested a small plate of cookies and a tall glass of milk, the glass sweating with tiny beads of moisture. A note had been left there:

In case you feel the need for something sweet between dreams.
~Mrs. C~

Jimmy smiled and turned his attention to a small dresser oppo-site the fireplace. There, folded in the top drawer, were several pairs of pajamas. He swapped his Lone Ranger apparel for a maroon set and found a dark green robe just his size hanging on the back of the bedroom door. Matching green slippers had been placed beside the dresser. Once changed, Jimmy discovered a cobalt blue glass with both toothbrush and tube of toothpaste within. He gathered the toiletries and left the bedroom in search of a sink.

The hallway beyond his bedroom door appeared to have lengthened in his brief absence. As he walked along, Jimmy noticed names on some of the many doors lining the walls, but not all. It took longer than he thought it would, but after passing dozens of doors and more than a few candles, Jimmy reached the end of the hallway. The bathroom was beautiful. A large pink porcelain tub stood on one wall, while the same colored sink stood opposite. The mirror confirmed that yes, indeed, he was quite tired.

After he had brushed his teeth and washed his face, Jimmy returned to his room. The fire had died a bit, and the walls were a softer shade of shadow. Jimmy placed his robe and slippers at the foot of the bed. Before he glided beneath the covers, he walked to the window, sat down inside the comfy nook and gazed out over the plaza below. He had no idea what time it was, but late or not, elves were literally everywhere he looked. They rode by in sleighs and atop reindeer or the occasional polar bear. Some zipped by on ice skates, while others rode specially-built bicycles for two, some-times three or four, which towed several more elves behind them at the end of long yellow tow ropes, atop brightly colored skis.

65

Jimmy could hear them laughing and cheering even from here in his little room high above.

Jimmy grinned and closed the curtains a bit, but not entirely. He guessed even Nurse Wilma would not mind tonight. A moment later he crawled into the bed and beneath the many covers. Just as he suspected, it was indeed the softest bed he'd ever felt. Jimmy lay there staring at the shadows dancing on the ceiling. He could hear the elves singing outside and music playing from somewhere in the house.

There was an occasional pop from the fire, a gust of wind or a boisterous laugh from the plaza—far sweeter sounds than the children or parents within the ward back home. There were no troubled coughs, no labored breaths, and no sobs in the dark. Here, laughter took the place of tears, and joy vanquished sadness. Despite his excitement, his delight and his wonder, Jimmy wished his parents could be here with him.

When he drifted off to sleep, Jimmy was greeted with magnificent dreams. His parents were happy again, his father even laughing from time to time, something Jimmy had not seen or heard for ages. He missed that more than anyone could imagine. Not only was his father laughing, but he had returned home from the horrible war, which was the most important thing. Jimmy was no longer sick, the children in the hospital were all better, and a world of magic lay ahead. They were some of the best dreams Jimmy had ever had.

CHAPTER 14

ALEXANDER

When Jimmy woke, he was almost afraid to open his eyes. The last thing he wanted to see was St. Joseph's, but he wanted to see his mother more than anything else and that meant the hospital again. Jimmy agonized over his emotions until he finally pulled the covers just below his nose and opened his eyes. As soon as he did, he realized that it had not all been a dream and that he was still a guest in the Claus home. Jimmy smiled. He would have such wonderful stories to tell his mother. They might even make his father laugh, just like in his dreams. At the prospect of exploring more of the North Pole's wonders and the magic permeating its every nook and cranny, Jimmy grew ecstatic. He even forgot how sick he was, which in itself was quite a feat considering how often the fact haunted him.

"Sleep well, Sir?" a small voice asked from somewhere within the room.

Jimmy jumped halfway out of the bed. As far as he knew, the room was empty!

"Sorry, Sir! Over here," the tiny voice said.

Jimmy glanced over at his nightstand. There, staring back at him, was a tiny brown mouse. He wore a green jacket and an ornate green cap, which boasted a red silk band, with crimson feather to match.

The little mouse bowed. "Pleased to meet you, Sir. My name is Alexander," he said, sweeping his hat in an easy graceful arc.

Jimmy rubbed his yes. "Hello?"

The tiny mouse straightened, placed his hat atop his head, and smiled. "Did you sleep well?"

"Umm... Yes, thank you!"

"Grand, grand. If I may... Your clothes have been cleaned and pressed. You will find them in the dresser. We also took the liberty of cleaning and polishing your boots," Alexander said.

"We?"

"Begging your pardon, Sir... we, the house guests."

Jimmy thought for a moment. "Oh, the stockings? On the banister leading upstairs! No wonder they were so small!"

"Yes, Sir," Alexander said. "The missus hangs them for us each year. She's a kind-hearted soul, that one."

"Yes, she is."

"I hope you are hungry, Sir," the little mouse said. "We began smelling the fruits and batter for hot-cakes not long ago. If I'm correct, I believe Jelly has outdone herself this time. And rest assured when I tell you that this is no small feat. Jelly's cooking equals even Krikin's, though she'd never admit to it."

Jimmy sniffed the air and welcomed the hunger pangs erupting in his stomach; they'd been missing during the mornings for a very, very long time. "I'm starving even though I shouldn't be. You wouldn't believe how much I ate yesterday!"

Alexander laughed. "Oh, I'm sure I have an idea, Sir. The elves love their food. If I may be so bold," the mouse dropped his voice to a whisper, "you can see it in good ol' Santa's waistline!"

Jimmy chuckled and studied the tiny mouse again, who smiled

back. "I'm sorry if I stare, Alexander; you're the first... well, you're the first talking mouse I've ever seen! Or met, or both actually!"

Alexander nodded. "Then it is my pleasure, Sir. But not to worry, things are a bit different here than say, well, anywhere else, as I'm sure you've gathered. It's no wonder you've never been able to understand mice before. Or birds, or dogs, or cats, or well, any other being that's not human."

"So Santa and the Elves can understand all of the animals here?"

"And we them! Though, most dislike the term *animals*, if you will permit me to say so. I think we've grown accustomed to the term *beings* as I mentioned before. It seems less, well, less animal-istic if I may."

"Oh I'm sorry, Alexander! I didn't mean to offend you."

The tiny mouse began to laugh. "No need to apologize, Sir! Now you best hurry off and wash up! The adventure of an Elvin breakfast awaits you!"

Jimmy raced off to wash for the day. When he returned, his bed was made and his clothes were laid out on the comforter. He offered Alexander a ride to the kitchen, which the tiny mouse accepted eagerly. He placed his new friend in his front shirt pocket, and the two went in search of Jelly's hot-cakes.

The living room was cheery as ever, and a new fire roared within the hearth. The sounds and smells of breakfast pulled Jimmy onward, and he stepped into the kitchen amidst a flurry of action.

"Well, good morning, Jimmy!" Mrs. Claus said, grinning. "I see you've met our old friend Alexander."

"good morning! And yes, ma'am," Jimmy replied.

Santa waved from the long table and folded a newspaper in front of him. "Good morning you two. What did you think of our new mattresses, Jim?"

"It was wonderful, thank you!"

"He slept like a hibernating bear, not to put too fine a point on it," Alexander said.

"Hello, Master Jimmy!" Jelly said as she raced by, her blue hair glowing bright. She'd tied little blue ribbons in it this morning; they, too, glowed bright.

"Good morning!"

Santa motioned to a chair next to him which faced the kitchen. "Come have a seat. Binks is off fetching some eggs, but he will be here directly."

Mrs. Claus sat a large glass of orange juice in front of Jimmy and filled Santa's mug with steaming black coffee. It smelled of vanilla.

"Alexander, would you like your usual, dear?" She asked.

Alexander was already halfway down Jimmy's arm to the table. "If you please, Miss," the mouse replied. He then scampered over to a miniature chair and table, sat down, unfolded a minuscule paper, and began to read.

"We've been working on those pillows and mattresses for some time now," Santa said. "A couple of young lads headed for NASA will find those plans pretty handy in a few years."

"Nah saw?" Jimmy asked.

Santa grinned. "The National Aeronautics and Space Administration, or NASA for short. They don't exist yet, so let's keep them a secret between us, shall we? Also, you'll have to forgive me, Jim. I'm not very good at keeping secrets, especially the big ones! I'm terrible at it, in fact. Let's just say you tested a product that won't see the light of day for a good forty, fifty years."

"Wow!"

"Indeed," Alexander said. "I've been sleeping on one of them for a year or two now. Quite comfy they are!"

Mrs. Claus returned to the table, and for a moment, Jimmy thought she was empty-handed. "Here you go, Alexander," she said. It was then Jimmy realized she held the tiniest tea cup he'd

70

ever seen, or had barely seen. How in the world she managed to hold it, much less keep it from spilling, was a mystery.

"Ahh, cheers," Alexander said.

Santa laughed. "Really, Alexander, you should try a good cup of joe just once."

Alexander grinned and took a sip of tea. "I will have to politely refuse, Sir. Unless of course the King, God save him, declares the national drink out of fashion! Or Churchill for that matter."

Santa smiled. "If I know Winston, I'd say he prefers the more..." He paused and glanced at Jimmy. "...robust refreshments, as it were."

Alexander and Santa laughed for a bit after that.

"You know my father was in England for a while," Jimmy said. "He's in France now, I think, maybe Germany. It's hard to get letters back and forth."

Alexander looked up. "England, you say? Whereabouts?"

"Devon, or North Devon, I think."

The mouse seemed to consider this. "I'm sorry, Sir; I don't believe I've had the opportunity to visit North Devon."

"That's ok, Alexander."

"Well, I guess we'll just have to take you with us this year, Alexander," Santa said, and winked.

Alexander's eyes widened. "That would be most kind, Santa!" "I don't think he would take up too much space, do you Jim?"

Jimmy shook his head. "No sir, not much at all."

"Unless of course you would rather visit that Henderson home you've been going on about. There's a family there again," Santa said.

Alexander's eyes widened and his tiny jaw dropped. "They've come back?"

"The elves tell me they have three young children as well," Santa replied.

Alexander placed his tea cup on the table and wrung his hands.

71

After a moment he stood, stared at his feet, and began pacing circles around the tiny table and chair.

Santa leaned over, cupped his hand, and whispered in Jimmy's ear. "The Hendersons have been a mystery for our little friend here for quite some time. I can't tell him yet, but he's on the right path, and given a small nudge now and then, he'll soon discover he has found his long-lost family."

"If you will excuse me, I must... I must return to the library at once!" Alexander said, and without any further adieu, he raced across the table and disappeared over the side.

Mrs. Claus sighed, smiled, and cleared the little mouse's table and chair from the table. "I'll ask one of the elves to send up his tea," she said, and walked back to the stoves.

"Lost family?" Jimmy asked.

"I've been helping Alexander for quite some time," Santa replied. "I found him in an old home, completely alone and quite injured. He's never been able to put together the entire mystery of his injuries, and what little he does remember about his family has been shrouded in mystery, as has that house—the Henderson home, as he calls it. The elves and I have been helping poor Alexander for years to try and answer some of his many questions. That home is filled with more magic than I've seen gathered in one place just about anywhere else outside of the North Pole."

"Wow. I hope there's something I can do to help him while I'm here," Jimmy said.

Santa smiled. "There might just be."

"Hello, hello, hello Master Jimmy!" a new voice rang out from across the room.

Jimmy turned and saw Binks bounce into the room carrying two large baskets of eggs. "Good morning, Binks!"

Just behind the elf, Krikin and Pimsy arrived along with Burgundy. Their coats and hats were covered in fresh snow, and their cheeks were fiery red.

"Good morning, Master Jimmy!" Krikin said, and waved. "And to you Mister and Missus!" he added towards Santa and Mrs. Claus. "…and to you Jelly, and you Binks, and well, everyone else present! Good morning to all, and to all a good day!"

Everyone greeted Krikin, who scampered off to help set the giant table.

For the next half-hour, more and more elves piled into the kitchen, dusted off, greeted everyone, introduced themselves to Jimmy, and took their seats. Jimmy learned that each week several dozen elves took turns spending a week's worth of mornings with the Clauses at their breakfast table. Every elf at the North Pole did this, guaranteeing each and every single one of them got a chance to break bread with their friends Mr. and Mrs. Claus. The elves would also swap cooking and baking duties from time to time, depending on when Mrs. Claus deemed an elf ready to go back and practice what they'd learned from her for a while before returning. The next week a different batch of elves would spend their breakfasts in the home, and so on and so on until the procession would start all over again.

Soon the table was filled with plates, utensils, cups of coffee, tea, orange juice, cider, and hot chocolate, not to mention surrounded by dozens of hungry bellies.

"Unless I'm missing something or someone, I think we're about ready!" Mrs. Claus said, and sat down along with Jelly and Binks.

Jimmy watched as stack after stack of hot-cakes floated through the air and placed itself on plate after plate after plate. Carafes of brightly-colored syrup floated overhead and sat themselves within arms' reach. Eggs of all kinds—fried, scrambled, and poached— arrived and seemed to know exactly which plate belonged to which person and who liked what.

"These are kiwi-blueberry, Master Jimmy! I like to call them klueberry! And that is mango-infused maple syrup!" Jelly said over the busy hum of cheerful diners.

"That sounds wonderful!" Jimmy replied. "What's a kiwi?"

An eruption of warm laughter broke out and filled the kitchen.

"Trust me, you'll enjoy it," Santa said, and winked.

And Jimmy did, more than any hot-cake he'd ever eaten.

CHAPTER 15

NORTH POLE TOURS

W hen everyone finished their second, third, and fourth helpings of Jelly's kiwi-blueberry hot-cakes, or klueberry as she liked to call them, the dishes washed themselves while the kitchen was cleaned by an army of animated brooms, rags, and mops. The elves all looked as if they'd hardly eaten a thing and talked excitedly over the day's schedule, including the gifts they were working on, the designs they hoped to create, and the decorations they were placing here, there, and everywhere it seemed. They also discussed Jimmy's upcoming tour at length, offering far more suggestions than possible, considering the amount of time each would take to accomplish. Santa and Jimmy made their way over to the kitchen's hearth while Krikin stoked the fire. After a time, most of the elves thanked everyone, excused themselves, and vanished off to wherever it was they were needed, worked, or wished to go. A far more quiet blanket seemed to cover the room.

"I should think he would want to see the workshops first!" Burgundy said.

"Oh, I suspect a ride on the new coaster should be first on the list!" Jelly replied.

"The coaster? The NEW coaster? After *that* breakfast?" Krikin asked. "Why, look at him! He looks ready to pop as it is!" the elf said, and added another log to the fire.

"Good point," Jelly replied.

"Why not visit the forest?" Binks suggested. "There's a new cub or two over in Polar Bear Square. I heard there was even a pink-furred cub!"

"Polar Bear Square! Oh, that would be so much fun! Or the ice park!" Pimsy added. "Or both! And don't forget the rose gardens! There are silver roses this winter!"

"Silver roses?" Jimmy asked.

Pimsy clapped her hands and bounced on the balls of her feet. "Silver indeed! I haven't seen a silver rose in over a decade. I wonder if I could convince one to grow in my hair with the rest of my primroses?"

"I hear there are some new baby reindeer as well," Mrs. Claus suggested.

"I knew Dasher and Snowbell were expecting, but I never thought it would be so soon!" Jelly replied.

Mrs. Claus shook her head. "Oh no, Snowbell and Dasher still have a few weeks yet. No, I believe this might be a part of Fireleaf's family."

"Fireleaf has a new member of the family, does he? I will have to stop in and say hello," Santa said.

"I just love reindeer babies!" Jelly said. The little elf's blue hair was glowing the brightest Jimmy had seen thus far. Jelly noticed his looks and smiled. "It's the blueberries!" she said. "Those are my favorite fruit ever, and as luck would have it, blueberry jams and jellies are my favorite things in the world to eat! Hence the name and the hair! Apparently, when I was younger, I ate so many blueberries and devoured so much blueberry jam that not only did my hair turn blue, but it began to sparkle and even glow a bright blue! So when my hair stayed that color, the name kinda sorta stuck!"

Jimmy chuckled. "That's great! I know a little girl who loves strawberries more than anything. She even has red hair."

"Oh, strawberries are one of my favorites!" Burgundy said.

"Maybe one day her hair will glow like mine!" Jelly said.

"There are the snow people to visit as well, let's not forget them!" Krikin said.

"Speaking of snow people, is Nix back yet?" Pimsy asked.

"Just last night," Krikin replied. "He was off visiting Master Walter and Master Steven again."

"He does love West Virginia, doesn't he?" Pimsy asked.

Krikin laughed. "That he does."

Santa took his pipe from the inside of his coat and lit it. "Why don't we ask Jim what he would like to do first?"

The elves all stopped and turned to eye Jimmy.

"I, uhh…" he started. "I would love to see the tree, the umm, the First Tree."

"That's a splendid idea, Master Jimmy!" Krikin said. "I could show you my new house!"

"That would be nice, Krikin; thank you."

"Why don't all of you take Jimmy on as many tours as he can manage, and I will meet everyone later?" Santa said. "I have several trips to make in the meantime. As long as Jim here doesn't object, that is?"

"Oh no, I am excited to see everything!"

"I told you," Krikin said, and nudged Pimsy.

"Well, I will leave you to it, then," Santa said. "Jelly, Binks, Jessica, breakfast was stupendous as usual!"

"Hear, hear!" the elves agreed. "Yes, thank you!" Jimmy said.

Santa excused Jimmy and the elves and continued to read his paper. Jimmy noticed the front page was covered in news about the war. Even here at the North Pole the Second World War made headlines. It was sad, tragic even, and Santa's expression agreed.

The elves helped Jimmy get ready and raced out the front door, but not before stuffing their pockets with cookies and candies. Snow was falling again, and the sky was a dark blueish black.

"Does the sun not rise here this time of year?" Jimmy asked as the troupe walked out onto the main street.

"Well, that's a tricky one!' Burgundy replied.

"Tricky, yes," Krikin agreed.

"You see, this place tends to move about quite often. We're not always at the North Pole, you understand," Pimsy said.

"The North Pole isn't always at the North Pole?" Jimmy asked.

The elves all giggled.

"The city isn't always at the North Pole, but the North Pole itself, well, it stays pretty much where it belongs!" Krikin replied.

"And to answer your question, Master Jimmy...." Jelly began. "We are at the North Pole now, and no, at this time of year the sun is almost always below the horizon. Hence all of the Christmas lights! Personally, I love this time of year in the North."

"As do I," Binks said. "Less ice and far more snow!"

"Here's to less ice!" Burgundy said. "I get so tired of slipping and sliding and gliding into things! I feel like an Elvin pinball sometimes!"

The group laughed.

"So no, we're not always at the North Pole," Krikin said.

Jimmy nodded. "I think I understand now."

"Good!" Burgundy said. "Just as an example, last week we were in Denmark, the week before that we were in Sweden, and last month we were in Finland for a time!"

"Wow! And the whole city moves?" Jimmy asked.

"The city, forest, homes, everything!" Binks replied. "But we always follow winter! It wouldn't do for some of us to get too warm, you see."

"Ahh. Like the snow people you mentioned? Who are they? Are they really made from snow?"

"That they are!" Binks said. "They're the embodiment of winter, you see. The souls, as it were. Some of them have been here longer than even the oldest of elves. They have such kind and warm hearts, even if they are made of ice."

"Nix showed me his heart once when I needed help," Jelly said. "It was beautiful, and it led me to exactly what I was looking for."

"And what was that?" Krikin asked.

Jelly smiled and her hair began to pulse blue again. "Well, that's something of a secret. But let me say, the snow people do indeed have the kindest and warmest hearts I've ever seen, or touched."

The elves led Jimmy down the street towards a long row of decorated buildings. Everywhere they went warm greetings came their way from passing elves. Several reindeer stopped and bowed, and a camel nodded hello. Jimmy was amazed at how warm he was. The snow and ice everywhere gave the impression that he should have been frozen solid in an instant, but he was quite cozy. The elves didn't seem to acknowledge the temperature at all and cheered as the snow began to fall in earnest for the first time that morning.

"Would you like to skate to the forest, Master Jimmy?" Pimsy asked.

"I umm…I'm not sure I know how, Pimsy."

"Oh, that's not a problem!"

"No, not at all!" Burgundy said. "We can show you in a jiffy! It's quite fun!"

Jimmy laughed. "Okay then?"

"Well, if we're to skate, we'll need a pair of boots for Master Jimmy," Krikin said. "Any thoughts on who should design his first?"

"Tobbler's?" Jelly asked.

"Minzer's?" Burgundy suggested.

"I've always loved my Vellrex skates," Binks said.

"Ooo!" Jelly said. Her eyes widened, "Vellrex!"

"I'm afraid I'm lost," Jimmy said.

Krikin chuckled. "Sorry, Master Jimmy—Tobbler, Minzer and Vellrex are all experts at crafting snow skates!"

"Snow skates? You mean ice skates?"

The elves chuckled for a moment.

"Oh, Master Jimmy," Krikin said. "I knew showing you all of our tricks would be fun! Ice skates are grand if you have enough ice, but not so fun if you run out! He then kicked at the deepening snow beneath their feet. No, snow skates are even better. You'll see!"

And so the elves and Jimmy were off to find snow skates, visit snow people, climb the first tree that ever grew, and more.

CHAPTER 16

CREATURES GREAT AND SMALL

J immy followed the elves onto a narrow side street. The snow was deeper here, so the group trudged along a bit slower. As they strolled, Jimmy made note of the numerous store fronts lining the narrow road. There were cheese shops, book stores, bakeries and at least two sweet shops whose store-front displays demanded a return trip if you could even manage to resist a visit at first glance. Some of the buildings were only a single story, while others stretched seven or eight stories into the sky. This particular street was just wide enough to navigate with a single sleigh, so almost everyone here was on foot. Further along, Jimmy began to notice covered walkways far above which connected one side of the street to the other via the taller buildings.

"I used to live just there," Krikin said, and pointed skyward.

Jimmy glanced up and saw a small balcony complete with tiny Christmas tree.

"You always did like the city life," Pimsy said.

Krikin smiled. "The city is wonderful! But I have to admit, I'm already excited to live in the Tree again after this year. Crendle says he expects it will grow at least two hundred more rooms this season."

"Two hundred! Really?" Pimsy asked.

Krikin nodded. "That's what he says!"

"The Tree grows...it grows...rooms?" Jimmy asked.

"Oh, yes!" Krikin said. "Ever since the elves began taking care of it, the Tree began growing homes for more and more of us each year! In return, we tend to its needs as they arise."

"You mean feeding and watering it?" Jimmy asked.

"Well, we've never really needed to feed or water it per se. But we did find that it loves music, specifically live song, so we do engage in a fair amount of singing when we sense it needs a good ballad or two."

"And stories," Burgundy added.

"Ahh yes, it does love a good story now and then," Krikin added. "You wouldn't be hard pressed to find an elf sitting by the fire, reading aloud a tale of adventure or romance deep into the wee hours of night."

"Music and stories," Jimmy said. "I wonder if my mother's plants would enjoy that?"

"I'd be shocked to discover they didn't, Master Jimmy," Binks said. "Utterly shocked! I read to my garden regularly, and you can tell a difference in the fruits and vegetables when I forget, or am called away on business."

"It's true," Jelly said. "A good season full of reading is a good season full of eating!"

Just then, Pimsy started clapping and skipping ahead. "Here we are! Here we are!"

Just ahead, the street opened up into a large circular courtyard with several streets leading away from it at all directions. In the center of the urban confluence stood an enormous building rivaling even Santa's home in sheer size. Its walls were build from polished white marble with sparkling silver veins coursing across their surface. They looked as if lightning had struck each and had frozen there for all eternity. The building's multi-level roof was constructed from a thick, light blue glass which appeared to resist any sort of snow or ice accumulation. As they drew closer, Jimmy could see millions of tiny snowflakes striking the roof and gliding off, never finding purchase. All about the sides of the building, cascades of snowflakes appeared as if white waterfalls flowed silently from the structure. Soaring stained glass windows stretched from the ground to the roof high above. Every second or two, the wonderful glass structures would explode in a dazzling display of colors as a mysterious brilliant light flashed into existence and then dissipated somewhere inside. A highly polished silver chimney issued forth pure white smoke which disappeared into the snow-laden clouds above.

"Wow..." Jimmy said as they approached. Another flash of light lit the windows, and he blinked away a tapestry of hues and intricate patterns which were suddenly embroidered on the inside of his eyelids.

"Master Vellrex built this himself!" Burgundy said. "I've always loved the glass rooftop."

"Me too!" Jelly said. "My favorite color."

"You don't say?" Binks replied, and nudged blue-haired elf playfully.

Jelly blushed, and her hair began pulsing with a deep cobalt light again.

"Shall we?" Krikin asked, and pushed on one of the two enormous silver doors.

When the troupe entered the building, Jimmy was confronted by the most amazing character he'd ever seen. A colossal blue and white dragon from the pages of nearly every fairytale he'd ever read stood before them. In its grip, the creature held an enormous boulder of what looked to be pure gold. He blew a dark purple flame onto the mass and molded the metal easily with enormous, clawed, sapphire-encrusted hands.

"Greetings, Master Vellrex!" Krikin said, bowing.

"Greetings, good tidings, and happiest of seasons, Master Vellrex! We are so, so happy to…" Binks started, and was calmed down by a smile and soft pat on his arm from Jelly.

Jimmy tore his eyes from the magnificent beast and saw that all of the elves were stooped in a low bow, their hats held to their chests. Jimmy followed suit.

The dragon turned his attention to Jimmy and the elves. "Sir Krikinfield, a pleasure as always." His voice was so deep it resonated in Jimmy's chest. He felt it more than heard it.

Vellrex placed the molten ball of gold into a large pool of water. Waves of white steam billowed up and out, and a long angry hiss echoed around the vast room.

"And hello Sirs Burgundrius and Binkrindrican. M'ladies Primrose and Jellendrial, it is a pleasure to see you, as always. I can only assume you've brought with you Master James?"

"We have!" Pimsy said, and straightened herself while fussing with the roses woven into her hair in a nervous and giddy motion. "Thank you so very much for seeing us! It's such an honor!"

Jimmy did not notice the elves finish their bows and remained bent at the waist until Krikin nudged him.

Jimmy jumped upright. "He-hello," he said. His cheeks were flushed, and his voice wavered. This was, after all, the first dragon he'd ever seen, and by the way the elves were acting, Vellrex was a creature to be respected. Jimmy seriously doubted his knowledge in etiquette for such an encounter. Vellrex seemed like royalty, yet he addressed the elves with Sir and Milady.

"Might we trouble you for a pair of snow skates, Master Vellrex?" Krikin asked. "We would very much like to show Master Jimmy the city and grounds, and…"

Jelly interrupted in her excitement. "…and Master Jimmy's

never skated on snow before, and well, your boots are by far the fastest ever designed! And well, well, we would very much like to teach him, and..."

Vellrex began to laugh. It was the sound of a colossal, yet friendly avalanche, and Jelly's hair began to glow brighter than Jimmy had seen yet. "M'lady Jellendrial, are you still keen to master some of my skates?"

"Yes, Sir, Master Vellrex, Sir...I would like to try... if it's not too much trouble...Sir...."

A deep rumbling chuckle filled the room and Vellrex smiled. "Why are you always so nervous around me, Jellendrial? Is it my size? Or is it that you are afraid I've heard of your last snow skating...adventure, shall we say?"

"I..." Jelly started.

The dragon grinned. "Tobbler's skates are very fast, M'lady, not to worry. I am aware of the skills one must possess in order to master them. You are not the first elf to find themselves in a bind out on the sea ice."

Jelly blushed and bowed again.

"Well, perhaps you are the first to find yourself so *far* onto the sea ice," Vellrex added, grinning. "Of course you may have a pair, M'lady. I've known for quite some time that you've been working up the nerve to come here and make your request. I've already constructed some of the magic for them, in fact, although I await your sizing and payment, as you know."

"You have! Oh thank you! We were hoping to visit the bookstore immediately, Master Vellrex!" Jelly replied.

The dragon smiled. "Good, good. And for you, Master James? Let's get a good look at your feet, shall we?"

Krikin motioned for Jimmy to step forward. Jimmy did as he was instructed, but it was clear he was nervous.

"Not to worry Master James," Vellrex said. "I've eaten already today, and you're a bit small for my likes," and added a good-natured wink.

The elves behind Jimmy broke into laughter, and the dragon smiled down at them in return.

"Thank you, Sir," Jimmy replied.

Vellrex chuckled, his voice filling the room and warming everyone. "If you please," the dragon said, motioning to what looked like shining blue pool of glass.

As Jimmy walked towards the circle, Vellrex blew a small fire out over the surface, liquefying the pools' contents.

"It's quite cool, I assure you," Vellrex said when Jimmy paused. "Simply remove your boots and socks and then step into the basin, if you please."

Jimmy did as he was instructed and stepped into the liquid glass. It was indeed cool as the mighty dragon had promised, and he watched in awe as the blue, honey-like liquid molded itself to the sides, tops, and bottoms of his feet. There was a moment of tiny gold swirls which sparkled and tickled Jimmy's toes within the liquid. After that, the liquid began to warm and finally crystal-lize. Soft musical chimes echoed up from the bizarre pool of fluid glass, and the liquid grew still.

"That should do nicely, Master James, thank you," Vellrex said. "Simply move your toes a bit, and you will be able to remove your feet in short order."

Jimmy wiggled his toes and then his feet. It tickled to do so, but soon he was able to step out as promised. Vellrex reached down, lifted the entire circle from the floor, and held it aloft. The magical liquid was now quite solid and, as light passed through it, Jimmy spied the outline of his bare feet and toes deep within. While he replaced his socks and boots, Jimmy glanced up to see Vellrex blow another purple flame across the disk of glass, which began to glimmer and glow. The dragon squinted at the object for a second more, inspected it further, and blew another small flame, this one dark red over the glass disk.

"Very, very nice," the dragon said after that. He turned the glass in his giant clawed hands. "Have the elves informed you of my price for such skates?" he asked, casting his brilliant eyes on Jimmy.

"I umm..." Jimmy started.

"Not yet, Master Vellrex. We only just thought of snow skates," Krikin said.

"Ahh, I see." The dragon gazed down at Jimmy. "In that case, Master James, I shall explain. I crave stories. Tales old or new, I enjoy them all. Adventure, romance, satire, I care not. Simply write a story for me, and we shall consider that payment in full. But..." the dragon paused, and his eyes seemed to sparkle. "I do have a special request, if you would indulge me?"

Jimmy cleared his throat, "I will do my best!"

Vellrex smiled, "Excellent. I would like to know more about you, and to hear the tale of your adventures with us thus far. Do that for me, and I will have your skates within the hour."

"You would like me to write a story about...well...me?" Jimmy asked, his cheeks were growing a hot red.

Krikin reached up and placed a reassuring hand on Jimmy's shoulder. "We'll have the tale for you lickity-split!" he called up to the dragon. "This is very kind of you!"

"Not at all, Sir Krikinfield, not at all. As for you M'lady Jellendrial, blueberry blue, I assume?"

The little elf's hair twinkled. "Yes, please!" Jelly said, and began to giggle.

"Sirs Burgundrius and Binkrindrican?" The dragon asked. "Are your skates performing as they should? Do you require any adjustments while you are here?"

Burgundy and Binks both shook their heads and assured the dragon that their skates were perfect. Binks even launched into a rambunctious tale of how much he loved his until, again, Jelly calmed him down. Vellrex just smiled and nodded in the polite manner which seemed to permeate his very being.

"And for you Master James? Of what color would you like your new skates?" Vellrex asked.

"I umm…" Jimmy started. "I…I would like whatever color you like, Sir."

Vellrex narrowed his eyes and smiled. "Interesting! I shall do my best then, Master James."

"Thank you very much!" Jimmy said.

"It is my pleasure, Master James" Vellrex said, then looked to the rest of the elves. "Now, off with all of you. I must begin work immediately if I am to produce your wares in time for you to use them on your adventures today! But first, Jelly, I must measure your tiny feet, if you please."

And with that, the little troupe smiled, bowed, and thanked the dragon profusely. Jelly pulled off her shoes and socks and skipped over to Vellrex.

CHAPTER 17

ELVIN WRITING 101

As soon as the group exited the wonderful building, Jimmy stopped.

"Krikin, I'm not sure I can write a story for Vellrex. At least, not a story that's good enough to pay for something like... like dragon-made snow skates!"

Krikin laughed. "Not to worry, Master Jimmy! We have faith in you, don't we?"

The elves all nodded and smiled.

"If I can write novels, then anyone can, Master Jimmy!" Burgundy said.

"I was... well, I was going to say the exact same thing!" Binks laughed. "I mean, well... Well, just listen to me! I'm a mess most of the time!"

Jelly patted the elf on the back. "You're just naturally excited, Binks! That's all. There's nothing wrong with being so happy so often that your tongue gets tied up with it all!"

"Thank you, Jelly-gel," Binks said. Now he was blushing.

"And Burgundy, I liked your last story!" Pimsy replied. "You're too hard on yourself."

Now Burgundy began to blush.

"Then it's off to The Bard of Avon!" Krikin said.

Jimmy shook his head, but smiled despite his concerns. If the elves said he could do something, then he was sure they were right. He had made gingerbread cookies, after all. Flying, dancing, magical gingerbread cookies, in fact! The memory reminded him of the treats he used to bake with his mother, before he was too sick to do so anymore. His heart sank, and he was sure he felt a small twinge in his chest which threatened to mature into a serious cough again. This thought produced a surge of panic which sprang to life somewhere in Jimmy's stomach and coursed through his entire body; it stopped in his heart and blossomed into fear. His father's voice echoed through Jimmy's mind. *"Control your fear, son. If you don't, it will control you."* That was the last thing his father had said to him before he left for war.

As he walked behind the elves, Jimmy did his best to fight the sadness now flooding over him. He fought with everything he had. If he did anything less, if he succumbed to the worries that had plagued him so viciously of recent, he might never feel happy again. So Jimmy tried to think of his mother and father while ignoring the harsh realities of his sickness as he did, and he tried to think of the elves and Santa while ignoring the prospect of returning to St. Joseph's sooner than he would like. These were by no means easy feats, but Jimmy tried; he tried for himself, for his parents and for his new friends. If he failed, if he let the sorrow overtake him, he would lose far more than he could bear. It was difficult.

It only took a few minutes for the elves to lead Jimmy to the bookstore. The front door was fashioned to appear as an oversized book with a shining gold title painted on the cover.

It read...

'Love's Labour's Won'

Krikin opened the door and a warm gush of book-scented air raced out into the cold street. The little elf smiled and ushered everyone inside.

Jelly began clapping and hopping about. "I think I know exactly what story to tell Master Vellrex!" she squeaked, and scampered off.

The bookstore was packed with just that. Books by the thousands lined shelves so tall and so wide they nearly disappeared into the building's rafters high above. Long brass ladders fixed with wheels top and bottom rolled about, with as many as four or five elves stacked on board, each probing the various shelves above. Giant gold chandeliers adorned with red and green candles hung from the ceiling, while one enormous double-sided hearth lit the remainder of the first floor. A floating company of unmanned instruments glided about the room playing soft, cheery music. Long plush couches and tall padded chairs dotted the area, each filled with elf after elf, reading or engaging in whispered conversation.

As Jimmy looked about, his gaze was pulled skyward. Dozens of catwalks crisscrossed over the main floor and over one another higher and higher. Along these footbridges, smaller bookshelves could be seen. It appeared not a single space of the enormous store was wasted. Even the ceiling boasted inverted bookshelves, packed to the gills with volume after volume. These were reached by the tallest of catwalks and ladders, not to mention the bravest of climbers.

"Shall we start your tale then?" Krikin asked.

"Sure?" Jimmy replied.

Burgundy, Binks, and Pimsy agreed to meet at the hearth soon, and each skipped off on separate paths in search of knowledge or adventure.

"I'll show you around a little, and then let's see if we can find The Bard," Krikin said. "If anyone at the North Pole can help you with your first novel, it's certainly him. Jelly's probably already found him in fact."

Krikin led Jimmy further into the busy library. The two squeezed down crowded aisle after crowded aisle and round elf after elf as Krikin described this or that. They passed half a dozen games of chess, several games of checkers, and one game that Jimmy did not recognize. It involved brilliantly colored gems and a larger playing surface than the chessboards allowed. Jimmy was keen to learn what it was, but first he needed to find this Bard fellow. The warmth inside the building coupled with the sounds of soft music and cheery yet muffled conversation helped Jimmy fight the fear which had surfaced in and around his heart.

After several minutes, Krikin finally stopped to ask directions. An older elf with a long yellow beard directed the two to a giant spiraling staircase near the rear of the main room. Krikin and Jimmy made their way to the flight of twisting steps and started up. When he thought they could climb no further, Jimmy noticed the stairs proceeded up and through the roof of the bookstore. When they emerged into what Jimmy could only guess was an attic, the two found themselves in a workshop of sorts. The lighting was dim here, mostly provided by tall white candles spread all about. Long, dark shadows stretched across the floor, danced up the walls, and glided over a ceiling of chocolate brown wooden beams. The air here smelled of leather, paper, and coffee. It was a cozy, comforting, quiet, and peaceful place.

Krikin lowered his voice to a whisper. "I should have guessed he'd be here."

The workshop was filled with beautiful writing desks. Before each desk rested a round padded stool, and on every desktop stood stacks of parchment and bottles of ink, and beautiful quills of various magnificent colors sat waiting. Beside all of these, each desk sported its own tall candle, which offered just enough light for the occupant to work by without interfering with the serene shadows throughout the room. Jimmy spotted Jelly chatting with another elf dressed from head to toe in glittering gold.

"There he is," Krikin said.

Jimmy looked to where Krikin had nodded and saw a tall, friendly-looking gentleman. His hair was dark, full of curls, and losing a battle of grounds with his shining forehead. A close-trimmed beard covered most of his face, and a silver earring hung from his left ear. He was busy reading a page from one of the elves' desks and nodding, a small grin just barely touching the corners of his mouth.

"Let's find you a desk first, and I'll go speak with Master William," Krikin said.

The two found an empty writing desk, and Jimmy sat down.

A large and somewhat intimidating stack of cream-colored paper rested before him. Next to it stood a writing quill nestled in a glass jar of dark blue ink. The tower of paper had to be three to four thousand blank pages tall, each of them just waiting for someone to bring them to life.

"Krikin, I don't think...."

"I'll just be a minute!" The little elf interrupted and skipped off.

Jimmy sighed and looked back at the towering stack of blank parchment. To think someone could take those pages and breathe magical life into them was...well, simply put, it was magical.

"You're Jim, yes?" a tiny voice asked from the desk opposite.

Jimmy looked up and noticed a little elf smiling back at him. She was a pretty thing, and far smaller than the other elves Jimmy had met; that, and she had wings!

"My name's Moth, but just about everyone calls me Mote. I'm a fairy, that's why I'm smaller and have these!" Mote said, and wiggled her tiny wings. "You were just thinking that, weren't you? That I was small? And if any of the other elves had wings?"

"I... I was, I..." Jimmy shook his head and cleared his stumbling throat, "It's nice to meet you Moth, erm, Mote," Jimmy said. "Yes, I was just thinking those things. You're…you're a fairy?"

"A fairy I am, Jim-Jiminy!" Mote said, and began laughing. "You look terrified, if you don't mind me saying?"

Jimmy nodded. "I've never written a story before; well, not a real story, anyway. I'm not sure what to do."

"Are not all stories real?" Mote asked. "Fiction or fact, I would think they're still as real as you or I!"

"Well, I meant, not a full-length kind of story. Not a complete one," Jimmy said.

"Ahh. Don't you fret, Jim-Jiminy. Even if a story is half-written, mostly undiscovered, or partially untold, deep in one's heart it's still a complete tale! At least for you anyway! And you've come to the very right place to tell your tale! Get it? See what I did there?" Mote said and chuckled. "Right? Get it? The right place? A writing place?"

Jimmy caught the joke after a moment and smiled. "Well, I hope that whatever I write, Vellrex likes it."

Mote's eyebrows rose and her little wings flittered. "Vellrex, eh? If Vellrex is reading your story, I assure you he will enjoy it. He's a dragon after all! Nobody reads like a dragon. No one at all."

"I sure hope you're right."

Mote let out a little giggle and looked back down at her work. "I am, Jim, trust me. I most certainly am."

"Sir Peterson! A pleasure to meet you," a new voice said.

Jimmy looked up to see Krikin and Master William smiling down at him.

"Hello, sir," Jimmy replied.

"Sir, is it?" The man asked. "Please, call me Will. I understand this to be your first novel?"

"Yes, sir, umm, Will."

"Then let's get to work, shall we? There's no better magic than that which resides within one's first novel. Nor is there stronger!"

Krikin cleared his throat. "If you both don't mind, I'm going to try and find a game of chess while the two of you weave your magic."

William nodded. "Not at all, Krikin. I hear Móin is still undefeated this month. You might attempt besting him."

"Is he now?" Krikin replied. "We'll have to see about that."

William chuckled. "Good luck!"

"Have fun," Jimmy said.

"Always!" Krikin said and skipped away.

William pulled a larger stool up to Jimmy's desk. "Krikin and Móin have been trading kings for years now. Never beat a dwarf at chess, lad; you'll never hear the end of it if you do."

"I'll try not to."

William laughed. "Well, let's see what inner muse you possess!"

"Sounds fun," Jimmy said.

William stomped his foot and clapped his knee. "Now that's what I like to hear! First, writing is a lot like baking! Krikin told me that you had your first go at Elvin baking last night. How was it?"

"It was wonderful."

"And did you try or taste your own work, as it were?"

"Yes, sir, er, Will."

"And what did you think? Was it worth all of the effort?"

Jimmy nodded.

"And if, say, I had some of your cookies...." William continued, and produced one of Jimmy's very own creations from his pocket., "...would you want me to enjoy your work as much as you enjoyed creating it?"

"Very much so!"

William took a bite from Jimmy's cookie and grinned. "Wonderful, lad, just wonderful. So why is writing like baking?"

Jimmy thought about that for a second. "Because you're creating something?"

William winked. "And because you bake not only for yourself but for others at times, yes? And when you bake, you don't always follow the directions, do you? You experiment here and there, yes? You're creating, just like you said! And what did Krikin tell you about baking? It's like what?"

Jimmy thought back. "It's like falling in love!"

"Exactly! If one can't write from the heart, one can't write at all," William said. "A broken heart, a wounded heart, a heart bursting with joy, it matters not. Without the heart, there can spring forth no tale worth telling." He let that bit sink in for a moment.

"No heart, no story." Jimmy said.

William smiled. "Precisely!" he said, and clapped Jimmy on the back. "So I understand Vellrex would like a story of your adventures here thus far?"

Jimmy nodded.

"So if you were to listen to your heart as it were, what kind of tale do you think it would tell of your adventures?"

"It would talk about the things that I love? Or maybe the things that scare me?"

"Exactly! Vellrex doesn't want an account of Santa's sleigh, or Elvin cookies. He knows both intimately. What would really be worth hearing however, is how you felt about those things! Love or no, tell him, tell us all how your heart experienced these events. How did you feel?"

"I think I understand."

"Good. Now for a little magic to go along with that understanding!" William said. "For starters, let's give your quill here a name." William pulled the tall, feathered pen from the bottle of ink and blotted it on a small, cream-colored cloth. "Everything with a soul has a name, yes? And if you're pouring your heart into something, it's best to make sure that that something has a soul just to be on the safe side."

"What about Excalibur?" Jimmy said without a moment's hesitation.

William's eyes widened, and Mote looked up from her work, her eyes equally wide, her mouth hanging open. She snapped it shut a split-second later and looked back down at her work, embarrassed.

William cleared his throat. "And what, pray tell, made you think of that?"

"I've always loved the stories about King Arthur, and, well... well...." Jimmy stopped.

"Well? Well what, lad?"

"You'll think it's silly. That I'm just being silly."

"Try me."

"Yes, try us!" Mote said, staring back at the two again.

Jimmy also cleared his throat. "Well, Excalibur was the mightiest sword ever made, but...well, it wasn't real! It was created by someone with a pen, right? So, if a pen created the most powerful sword ever written about, and if the pen is mightier than the sword, then it seems like I should call my pen Excalibur."

William and Mote sat in stunned silence.

"Told you you'd think it was silly."

William smiled and placed a gentle hand on Jimmy's shoulder. "Quite the opposite, lad. That was...that was profound! Many wearing rapiers are afraid of goose quills, indeed."

"Anyone can draw a sword, Jim-Jiminy. Few can draw emotion with strikes of ink and thrust of quill!" Mote added.

Jimmy let out a deep a sigh of relief.

"And if I may, never be afraid of what others might think of your writing. It makes for poor stories," William added.

"Okay."

William handed Jimmy his pen. "Now tell the pen its new name, and ask it politely if it will go on an adventure with you."

Jimmy stared at the quill and then held it in front of him. "Hello, Excalibur. Would you like to help me tell a story?"

In an instant the pen began to glow and lurched from Jimmy's grasp to dance in the air above the stack of parchment.

"Wow!" Jimmy said.

"Now all you have to do is tell Excalibur your tales! And by that, I mean just remember them, and it will do all the work. Try it out for a bit and see if I'm right. I'll be back shortly to inspect your progress."

"And I'm here if you need me," Mote said.

"Thank you both," Jimmy said.

William nodded and left to assist others, while Jimmy began to recall the events of recent. The pen did just as William said it would, and began writing page after page at any hint of a thought which Jimmy had. And never, not once did Jimmy have to even touch the magical quill. It even dipped itself into the ink when necessary. The paper also acted on its own, flipping when necessary, stacking itself when filled, and replacing itself one page after the next. After a while, the act of this new way of writing became so comfortable and so natural that Jimmy closed his eyes and did his best to tell the magnificent dragon next door the finest story he'd ever heard.

CHAPTER 18

A BARD IN ALL OF US

When Jimmy completed his story, he opened his eyes and was shocked to see the pages of finished work he and Excalibur had managed. A stack nearly three inches high stood next to an almost empty bottle of ink. Jimmy would have sworn the pen looked tired, exhausted even. He also took note of the sadness which had filled his heart recently, and how little of it remained there now. It was as if he'd used his magical pen to purge the sorrow from his very soul. He hoped the story wouldn't sadden Vellrex, though; the last thing he wanted to do was pass along his pain and fear to anyone else, especially a dragon! The idea of saddening a dragon seemed somehow far more than just cruel, it seemed unforgivable.

"Móin is getting better at his defense," a familiar voice said from behind. "It's pretty good now, actually."

Jimmy turned to see a smiling Krikin.

"But not quite good enough," the elf finished with a chuckle. "Is that your story?"

"I think so," Jimmy replied. "How long have I been working?"

Krikin withdrew a tiny watch from his front pocked. "About twenty minutes I should think."

"Twenty minutes?" Jimmy asked and looked back at the stack of finished pages. "That's it?"

Krikin shrugged. "Maybe twenty-three?"

"Gee wiz!"

"Let's take it over to Master William and see if we can't get it bound!"

Jimmy stood and gathered his new book. "It was nice to meet you, Mote."

The fairy looked back up and smiled. "We'll see each other again, Jim, don't you worry about that!"

"Hiya Mote," Krikin said and offered a little wave.

"Kriky," the fairy replied and buried her face back into her work in a somewhat fumbled hurry.

"Oh, and don't forget your new pen!" Krikin added, and pointed back to the desk.

"My new pen?"

"You named it, didn't you?" the elf asked. "Well, yes, but...."

"Then it's yours! Hurry up now. Do you want pictures for your book? They have an amazing set of paintbrushes here."

"If we have time," Jimmy said as he took Excalibur. "I'm not too sure I can draw all that well, or paint."

Krikin laughed. "Come now, Master Jimmy! You've learned to bake the Elvin way, and now you've learned to write the Elvin way. What makes you think drawing, or painting would be any different? It's just a new set of skills to learn, that's all!"

Jimmy smiled. "I guess you're right. But on second thought, I'm not sure my story really needs pictures."

Krikin grinned and nodded. "Write well enough, and no artist can create a picture half as grand as the art that words paint on the canvas of one's mind."

"I like the way that sounds," Jimmy said.

"It's true!" the little elf replied.

They found William, and he too looked surprised at the size of Jimmy's new book.

"Such a lengthy tale for a first effort. I am impressed!" William said. "I would be honored to read it, if you would allow me the privilege."

Jimmy shrugged. "I just tried to tell a good story. Anyone who wants to read it can, I guess."

"Not worried what others might think or say?" William asked.

"No, not really. If they like it, they like it, and I'm glad! If not, well, they sure have their pick of other books in this building," Jimmy said.

William and Krikin broke into laughter.

"That they do, lad! That they do," William said. "I will have a copy made immediately. I assume you would like it bound?"

"Yes, please," Jimmy said.

"And have you thought of a title?"

Jimmy cocked his head to the side and thought for a moment. "How about *The Elves*?"

Krikin cleared his throat and blushed.

William grinned. "That sounds fine! It's your book, after all; only you can give it a name. *The Elves* it is!"

"Thank you, but...but I don't...well, I don't have any money, sir, umm Will."

"That's good, because neither does anyone else here! We survive on a sort of barter system. I help you, you help me, understand?" William asked.

"I think so. But I'm not sure I have anything to offer you?"

William simply held Jimmy's book aloft and raised his eyebrows.

"Oh. Well, you can have a copy if you'd like," Jimmy said. "I mean, I'm not sure I could have written it without you."

William smiled. "Oh, you could have written this and far more

101

without my help, lad. But thank you; I would very much like to place a copy here in the library for others to enjoy. That will be payment enough. I shall have the book copied and bound here in the next minute or so. Oh, and before I forget, take this."

William handed Jimmy a small rectangular wooden box with the name "Excalibur" engraved in elegant script on the lid.

"Wow," Jimmy said, and opened the container. The inside was lined in purple felt and decorated with gold embroidery.

"For your pen. Don't forget, these quills are quite fragile, so take good care of them. And most importantly, remember that they have a life of their own, and will give life to your tales if you let them! Lastly, like any living breathing thing, your pen will need nourishment! Simply feed it stories from your heart, and that will be more than adequate."

"Thank you very much."

"Not at all. Doesn't Jelly have an order to place as well?" William asked.

"Yes, she does, Master William, and I think she's on her way over now, by the looks of it," Krikin replied.

Jimmy turned to see the blue-haired elf speeding towards them with an enormous stack of parchment in her hands and an even larger smile spread across her face. As usual her hair glowed bright.

"Wow!" Jimmy said when she arrived.

Jelly laughed. "I've wanted to tell this story for a while now!"

"I'll say," Krikin said.

"Well, I also knew we should hurry, so that's why it's so short," Jelly said.

"Short?" William asked. "I would wager that's the largest work I've seen in some time. Is it illustrated as well?"

"Oh no, I have another book idea for illustrations. This one's just good old-fashioned print and nothing else!"

"Might we inquire as to the subject?" William asked.

"Certainly! It's a cookbook for dragons, with stories thrown in for good measure!" Jelly answered. "Mrs. Claus and I have been talking about it for ages now."

"Well, that would explain the size," Krikin said.

William laughed and clapped his hands. "A gargantuan cookbook, for giants! Fitting."

"You know, that's not a half bad title!" Jelly said.

"Well, let's have it Jelly, and I'll get it bound along with our new friend's book," William said.

Jelly handed over her towering stack, and William nearly lost the entire handful.

"I'll find you shortly!" he said from behind the tower of paper, and stumbled off in search of a clear place to set Jelly's cookbook and *The Elves* before they ended up all over the North Pole.

"I saw Burgundy, Binks, and Pimsy down by the cider station," Jelly said.

Krikin chuckled. "Let's go find them before Burgundy ends up having a few too many."

"Oh, I'm so so excited to try a pair of Vellrex's snow skates!" Jelly squeaked. "So what was your story about, Master Jimmy? Oh wait, Vellrex wanted to hear of your adventures, didn't he? Did you have fun writing them?"

"I sure did!" Jimmy replied.

"Good! If it's no fun to write, then it's no fun to read! That's what I always say."

Burgundy, Binks, and Pimsy were exactly where Jelly said they would be. All three stood about an enormous brass carafe, each holding a steaming cup of pungent cider and chatting away. A small handwritten sign hung from the shining lid.

TODAY'S CIDER CREATED
BY
MISSES LAVENDER BLUE-ROSE
THE EXACT INGREDIENTS ARE SECRET!
FEEL FREE TO GUESS, BUT STOP ASKING,
'CAUSE WE'RE NOT TELLING!
ENJOY AND THANK YOU!

Several tiny notes had been taped around the sign. All of them, guesses as to what special ingredients had been used in the magnificent cider.

"I'm telling you..." hic "...they've added orange..." hic! "...zest today..." hic! hic! "...I can taste it!" Burgundy said between happy hiccups.

"I think you're right, and there's something else, something I can't – quite – place..." Binks replied. "It's almost, almost flowery, like, like...." The little elf shook his head in frustration, took a sniff from his cup, and followed this by another contemplative sip and loud gurgle.

"ROSES!" Pimsy shouted! This drew several stares and at least one chuckle.

Burgundy, having spilled some of his cider at Pimsy's outburst, raised his eyebrows and took another sip. "I think you're right!" hic! he agreed. "Orange zest and rose petals! BRILLIANT!" hic! hic!

Jimmy and Krikin joined their friends, and by the time they had all finished their third, fourth, and in Burgundy's case ninth cups of cider, William reappeared with Jelly's and Jimmy's new books. Each was bound in extravagant-looking cloth and wood.

"*The Elves* for James, and Jelly's *The Gargantuan Cookbook for Giants*," William said.

Everyone thanked William and, with new books in hand, the

troop was off. Jimmy was positive he heard several whispers as they left and saw more than one elf approach William and point back towards him and his new friends. He hoped again that his story was a good one.

CHAPTER 19

DRAGONWEAR

Vellrex was absent from the main chamber when Jimmy and the elves returned. But thunderous rumblings emanating beneath their feet told them the dragon had not gone far at all.

"Either that's Vellrex down there, or the cider I drank!" Burgundy said.

Everyone laughed.

"You'd think there was alcohol in that cider the way it affects you, Burgundy!" Binks said between giggles.

Burgundy chuckled. "I just love apples, that's all!" hic!

"That's one word for it!" Pimsy said.

The group snickered some more.

"I wonder if he's done yet," Jelly said while clasping *The Gargantuan Cookbook for Giants* to her chest. She was obviously excited and could barely contain herself.

"All good things, Jelly, all good things," Binks replied.

"Does Vellrex live here as well?" Jimmy asked.

"That he does, though he travels quite often," Krikin answered. "He was gone for about four, maybe five years once. Santa said he was tending to relatives, and looking for clues to Alexander's past."

"That's when Tobbler and Minzer started making skates and dragonwear," Pimsy said.

"Dragonwear?"

"Oh yes, Vellrex shared his designs with the two before he left, and they've been trying to master his plans ever since," Pimsy explained. "Snow skates are just one of the things made with dragon scales. Santa's sleigh, for instance? The runners? They are lined with them as well. A gift from Vellrex and Krymson."

"Who is Krymson?" Jimmy asked.

"Krymson is Vellrex's brother. He lives near the First Tree actually. Maybe we'll see him today!"

"I'm afraid Krymson is in Europe at the moment," a deep voice said from the rear of the main room.

Jimmy turned and saw the dragon's giant head rising up from a large opening in the stone floor. Vellrex climbed into the room until finally the entire massive blue giant stood before them.

"Santa asked Krymson to protect some of the troops," Vellrex said. "You know Krymson and war, always willing to fly right in. Alas, these are not appropriate topics for conversation on such a special day. Have you brought payment for my wares?"

"We have, Master Vellrex!" Jelly replied as she rose from her bow.

Jimmy had not caught the elves bowing, as his gaze had been transfixed on the mighty dragon climbing up through the floor. In an effort to correct the slight, he bowed low, said hello and almost dropped his new book. Vellrex chuckled and inspected the troupe. It was the first time Jimmy noticed the dragon's eyes. They were bright blue surrounded in what looked to be liquid purple flame. They were mesmerizing.

"William was nice enough to help me with this," Jimmy said, and stepped towards Vellrex holding his story aloft.

The dragon took the book with one graceful move of his giant hand. *"The Elves,"* Vellrex said as he inspected the cover. "I am honored by your gift, Master James." He then blew a bright purple flame across the book in his hand, and Jimmy's voice began echoing about the room. For a moment dragon, elves and young boy alike stood and listened to part of Jimmy's tale, told by none other than the author himself. To Jimmy's surprise the book did not burst into flame as he expected; it simply glowed and read itself aloud.

"That sounds splendid, Master James," the dragon said, and in an instant, the phantom voice faded away. "I look forward to hearing the rest!"

Jelly bounced up next to Jimmy and held her cookbook aloft as best she could. Vellrex's eyes widened, and he took the book to examine.

"Such a large..." Vellrex paused. "A cookbook indeed!" he said, and began to laugh. "A thousand thanks, M'lady Jellendrial."

"My pleasure, Master Vellrex!" the elf said.

Again the dragon blew purple flame across the book he held, and Jelly's voice began echoing off the walls.

"...It's no easy thing to blend oranges and grapes after all! Especially for jams and syrups! One must always be mindful of seeds and the occasional peel," the elf's disembodied voice instructed.

Vellrex grinned. "Oranges and grapes, you say?"

Jelly's voice faded away.

"My appetite grows just thinking of it," the dragon said.

Vellrex sat the books on a large crystal table and reached into a round pool of silvery mist. Jelly and Jimmy both gasped upon seeing the snow skates Vellrex retrieved. So did Krikin and the rest of the troupe.

"For you, M'lady," Vellrex said, and handed the small elf a glimmering set of sapphire and amethyst boots.

"Sir, I...Master Vellrex...I..." Jelly said, and tears began to spill out over her rosy cheeks. "I..." she tried again, but her voice cracked, and she stumbled over an inconvenient lump which now held purchase halfway down her little throat.

Vellrex just smiled and bowed his head low.

"And for you, Master James," the dragon continued after a moment, handing Jimmy a set of brilliant purple skates. "These are Tyrian-purple, a dye from several sea-snail friends. When I was young, the color was very rare indeed, and rather expensive. But even with today's technology and the magic some possess, I consider the original dye superior in color. I hope they are to your liking."

Jimmy marveled over his skates and the mystical way in which the light appeared to dance about the mesmerizing purple color. "Yes, sir, thank you very much!"

"I...These are wonderful, Master Vellrex!" Jelly finally managed. She wiped away several tears, and the smile which now covered her entire face threatened to engrave itself there permanently.

Vellrex bowed again. "Now off with you all. The morning is young, so are you, and wondrous adventure awaits!"

Jimmy and the elves bowed again and left the dragon pondering his new books. The group stopped outside the shop and turned to face one another as Jimmy's voice again echoed within the walls of the dragon's beautiful home.

"Those are magnificent!" Krikin said as Jimmy and Jelly inspected their skates. "That reminds me!" he added, and whistled.

Burgundy, Binks, and Pimsy all whistled into the air as well. Seconds later, four sets of empty snow skates glided down the street and came to rest beside their corresponding owner. Each set of skates was a different color; Burgundy's boasted orange with yellow lighting bolts on the sides.

"They look, they look so nice, but..." Jimmy said and turned his new boots over to inspect the soles. "How do they, I mean, I don't see any wheels or blades?"

The skates appeared to be simply boots; very decorative and ornate boots with deep tread for ice and snow, but nothing more.

"Ahh, but watch!" Krikin replied, and stepped out of his regular boots and into his emerald green skates. As soon as he did a soft emerald light appeared beneath the soles. Krikin rose two to three inches above the snow. A tiny hum drifted out from beneath the elf's skates.

"Neat!" Jimmy said, and sat down, eager to put on his new skates.

The rest of the elves followed suit, setting their regular boots aside. Jimmy pulled on his skates and was amazed at how warm they were, not to mention comfortable. They seemed to massage his feet from the moment his first toe entered.

"They will adjust themselves when you stand up. That's why there are no laces or buckles," Krikin said.

Jimmy stood and felt himself rise above the snow. And just as Krikin had promised, the boots tightened themselves snug.

"They sure are warm!" Jimmy said.

"Dragon scales never completely cool," Pimsy replied as she, too, stood and hovered above the snow. Her skates were a bright blonde color with tiny yellow primroses painted on the sides. They matched her hair perfectly.

Beneath each set of skates a colorful glow matching the color of the corresponding skate now illuminated the snow.

"Neat," Jimmy said.

"Now before we show you how they work, let's send these fellows home," Krikin said, and pointed to the discarded footwear. "Repeat after me, Master Jimmy:"

Boots go home!
Go rest! Don't roam!
Boots get dry! Go quick! Now fly!

Jimmy repeated the limerick and watched his boots, along with the others, take flight and disappear over the rooftops.

Krikin nodded his approval. "I'll teach you the whistle to get them back later."

"And now for some skating lessons!" Jelly said, circling easily around Krikin and Jimmy. "Have you ever tried ice skating or roller skating, Master Jimmy?"

Jimmy shook his head to indicate that he had not. "I've seen pictures, but I've never really tried."

"Well, it's really pretty simple! Actually, snow skating is far easier in my opinion, but let's get you started. All you have to do is point your feet slightly to the sides, toes out, and sort of, well... Kick off one foot at a time! Like this!" Jelly said and pushed from her right foot, then left, and glided away. A small glowing blue trail followed her.

For the next several minutes the elves taught Jimmy everything they knew about snow skating. Jimmy learned with amazing speed, and in less time than it took him to write a novel for Vell-rex, he was gliding up and down the street with ease. A few minutes more and Jimmy was able to skate backwards just as easily as forwards.

"This is fun!" he said, and glided by Krikin. The elf laughed and cheered him on.

"Better than walking, isn't it?" Burgundy asked.

"So much better! And it's easy!" Jimmy replied and promptly collided with a snow bank. When he dug himself out, he laughed until his sides hurt, then laughed some more.

CHAPTER 20

THE FIRST TREE

S now skating proved to be one of the most exciting activities Jimmy had ever experienced. He found that with a little patience, and a dash of confidence, he could accomplish stunning maneuvers and complete some of the more intricate tricks which the elves showed him. Gliding on a cushion of dragon magic over freshly fallen snow was like hovering above cotton ball clouds with Aladdin's magic carpet. It was divine.

Jimmy and the elves made their way through the enormous city and out one of the many gates. Once beyond the walls, the First Tree could be seen from just about everywhere when there was a break in the snow or a shift in the wind. It wasn't until Jimmy spotted it from the ground that he truly appreciated its massive size. The forest surrounding the Tree was still far off in the distance, but the open terrain allowed the elves to teach Jimmy a thing or two more about his skates and speed.

Before long, the troupe was gliding over rolling snow banks and zipping across frozen lakes and streams. Aside from Dasher's amazing speed, Jimmy thought perhaps this was the fastest he'd ever traveled. Burgundy was especially fond of taking to the air as he launched himself off large drifts or outcroppings of ice when he could find them. Pimsy was a more graceful skater, content to smile and hum a tune as she traveled, her hands clasped casually behind her back, while Krikin, Jelly, and Binks helped Jimmy and chatted excitedly over their planned destinations.

Soon they entered the great forest surrounding the First Tree. Everyone slowed, and Krikin led the group to a well-manicured path which snaked in and out of the trees. The trail was lined with tall gas lampposts which cast amber pools of light upon the bluish-white ground. Some posts were decorated in red and white ribbon, others were strung with colorful garland, and a few were decorated as if they were Christmas Trees themselves. The extra light they provided was a beautiful addition to the cool blues and grays from the snow and ice as well as the dark rich jades and earthy browns of the forest. The aromas here were as rich as the Claus's kitchen. Deep pungent pine and wonderful woody scents coupled with the faint aroma of ice and snow were intoxicating.

As he glided through the forest, Jimmy noticed there were homes within its boundaries, not just on the outskirts as it appeared from the air. These cottages were just as impressive, and more than one looked to be a picture-perfect replica of the fabled gingerbread house from *Hansel and Gretel*. Jimmy almost collided with a large pine as he craned his neck to get a better look at one of the sugary-looking abodes. He had been given an illustrated storybook of the tale when he was younger, and even now the book waited for him back at the ward. The thought of returning to the hospital frightened him again, so he quickly pushed the idea away while tearing his eyes from the magnificent and delicious-looking home.

As they moved deeper into the forest, more and more elves appeared, and decorations began popping up on the trees and grounds. Occasionally, Jimmy had to stop himself from staring lest he collide with a snow bank, snow-covered hedge, lamppost, or tree. The path soon widened, and a clearing came into view just ahead.

When the friends entered the glade, they were confronted by one side of the enormous First Tree. It towered upwards so far that Jimmy could not make out its lowest branches, only snow-burdened clouds. This time he failed at avoiding an icy collision as he craned his neck and eyes skyward.

Jimmy laughed as several pairs of hands pulled him out of the snow bank which had stopped his travels like some frozen pillow.

"Impressive, isn't it?" Krikin asked.

Jimmy chuckled and wiped himself off. "I'll say."

Krikin smiled and whistled a little tune. A moment later his regular boots burst through the trees and sat themselves by his feet.

"Let's teach you that whistle, Master Jimmy!" Krikin said. "Just whistle and wish your boots to come back. It's really that simple. But, you have to *want* them to come when you do, like calling a favorite pet!"

Jimmy thought of his uncle's dog, Rocket. He wished for his boots to come back, licked his chilled, dry lips, and whistled. Sure enough, the boots Santa had given him flew into sight and plopped down at his feet.

"I wish I could do that back home," Jimmy said.

Krikin smiled, but Jimmy caught that same worried expression the elf had displayed the previous night, hidden just below the cheery exterior. "You never know, Master Jimmy, maybe you can."

When everyone was back within their original boots, they sent the snow skates home to rest and trudged across the glade. The snow was falling hard now, and the ground was getting more and more difficult to navigate. It was tiring work, but the sheer beauty of their surroundings made the trek a lovely one, and no one minded the effort. Jimmy noticed that Pimsy and Jelly could walk on top of the snow, barely leaving footprints, whereas he, Krikin,

Burgundy, and Binks all sank knee deep in the icy fluff. As the group grew closer to the Tree, Jimmy spotted a small door carved into the bark, then another, and after a moment, dozens and dozens of doors could be seen lining the bottom of the tree, each with a small window and brass doorknob.

Krikin walked over to one of the doors and opened it; warm amber light spilled forth to greet them. "Welcome to the First Tree, Master Jimmy!" he said, and ushered everyone inside.

The interior of the tree was warm and bright. The wood was golden yellow and polished to a bright sheen. The first room they found themselves in was perfectly round, and all about the walls, coats and caps of every color hung on decorative brass hooks. Two small fires burned bright and hot on opposite sides of the room. From what Jimmy could tell, the flames had no effect on the wood from which the hearths were carved and the smoke, if there even was any, was absent.

"I think maybe we should... well... you know... surprise Master Jimmy at the top..." Binks said, and winked to Krikin.

Krikin cocked his head and stopped removing his coat and cap. He smiled, pulled his coat back on, and resituated his cap. "I think you're right, Binks!"

"Ooooo!" Jelly said and grinned.

The elves all beamed at one another.

"A surprise, huh?" Jimmy asked and smiled.

Pimsy bounced and giggled. "You'll love it! But keep your coat and cap with you."

"Well, let's get going!" Krikin said. "Lots to see!"

The elves led Jimmy out of the first room and into a much larger area. Here, dozens of beautifully carved elevators were hard at work within a shining brass grillwork. The elevators themselves were carved from amber wood and accented with polished chrome. Each was occupied by anywhere from one to a dozen elves.

115

"Beats the stairs, that's for sure," Burgundy said.

"And more fun, too!" Binks agreed.

Krikin walked over to one of the elevator shafts and waited for the intricate grillwork to open. After a brief pause, a cart glided into position before them. Several elves said hello as they exited and the troupe piled in.

"Where first, Master Jimmy?" Krikin asked.

"I umm…"

"I know! The first toyshop!" Pimsy said.

Krikin's eyes widened. "That's a great…wait…do you suppose we should wait for Santa?"

"I don't think he'd mind, Krikin," Jelly replied.

"Nor I," Binks agreed.

"Then it's settled!" Krikin said, and pressed a small, glowing button.

Jimmy looked up into the distant scaffolding and was surprised when the elevator plummeted downwards. Since the framework was grilled, and the elevators themselves were designed in similar fashion, Jimmy could look out of not only the walls, but the ceiling and floor as well. Beneath his feet a dark shaft engulfed the cart for a moment, and far below, a warm yellow light came rushing up towards them, or they down to it—it was difficult to tell from within the deep shadows.

A cool rush of wind crept through the floor and out over their heads, threatening to pull each of their caps from their snug purchases. The dim shaft in which they found themselves soon disappeared, and the cart descended through an enormous cavern, its ceiling festooned in polished roots and catwalks.

"We're underground now?" Jimmy asked.

"Oh yes!" Jelly said. "Santa decided that his first workshop should be near the First Tree's beginnings, so he started here! Close to the Tree's heart!"

"I thought the North Pole was built on a layer of ice? Shouldn't we be underwater?"

"Not here, no, but in some places the North Pole is actually built on an ice sheet! Remember, we move around quite a bit. And some areas never move, just the sections around them! The First Tree is one of those places that remains in the same location; we just sort of move around them."

Jimmy's brow furrowed, his lips pursed, and his head cocked to the side. "So how do you...I mean, how can you...how is it possible to find your way from one place to the next if the places you're going and the places you're leaving move around sometimes?"

"Simple!" Jelly replied. "Elf paths! The shortest distance between two points is not always a straight line, after all! Sometimes they're squiggly, sometimes loopy, and sometimes they're not even lines at all! Not when you have a little magic on your side, that is."

Jimmy shook his head and decided it best not to attempt a better understanding. He concluded that from time to time a thing just is, and that's about as much understanding as you need.

"Well, it sure is amazing!" Jimmy said, and gazed about.

"Just wait," Jelly replied, and bounced her little blue eyebrows.

The elevator came to a stop, and its doors opened onto the largest enclosed space Jimmy had ever seen. It was so vast that he could not discern an end in sight no matter where he turned. Thousands upon thousands of elves hurried to and fro, engaged in everything from wrapping boxes of all size to painting various ornaments.

"Tours are from noon 'till three, Krikin, ya know that!" a voice said from just ahead.

"Hello, Crendle!" Krikin replied.

Jimmy spotted an older, bearded elf standing atop a tall platform surrounded by levers of all sorts and just as many lights and gauges.

Small bursts of steam billowed out of brass pipes which encircled the platform, and tiny whistles squeaked away. The elf studied the group with narrowed eyes below an impressively gleaming bald head and appeared to be on the verge of further admonishment.

"Oh, ya've brought Master Jimmy!" Crendle said after a moment, and raced down from his intricate platform and over to the group.

"I thought an early tour would be all right, considering our guest," Krikin replied.

Crendle smiled. "Of course! Of course! It's a pleasure to meet ya, Master Jimmy!"

"Hello," Jimmy said as Crendle shook his hand.

"I heard ya might be stopping by, but I assumed Santa would be bringing ya. My apologies!" Crendle said. "And hello Jelly, Pimsy, Binks, Burgundy."

The elves all smiled.

"Well, come on then! Have a look at my new monitoring station! It still needs a few adjustments, but so far, she's been handling herself quite well!" Crendle said, and led them over to his platform where they climbed up to a kind of control station.

Crendle pointed to the various railings and latticework. "Mind the framework, Master Jimmy. It's steam-powered, ya know, and a bit warm at times."

Jimmy nodded.

Krikin patted the older elf on the shoulder. "Thank you, Crendle. I was wondering if the new Bounders were up and running?" he asked. "I thought they would be a first-rate method of touring the factory." A mischievous grin flooded across his face.

Crendle's eyes narrowed and began to sparkle. "Oh they're up, so to speak!"

Jimmy craned his neck and saw what it was Crendle and Krikin were discussing. Nearly one hundred feet in the air hung a massive brass corral. It looked like an enormous inverted basket, and within it, floated a dozen or so gigantic multi-colored balloons. But these balloons were like no other Jimmy had seen. They were wrapped in pearly white netting which culminated in a sort of woven seat beneath each balloon. The seats themselves were constructed of both rope and wood, with flight sticks fashioned to the arm rests. At least that's what Jimmy guessed them to be, for on the sides of the contraptions, wooden propellers had been fastened, and dorsal fins jutted from the rear of each.

"They look just like I imagined!" Krikin said.

Crendle nodded and pressed a button on his control panel. Next to Jimmy, a brass gate closed off the station, and the entire platform bolted up into the air towards the Bounder corral. Tiny puffs of steam and musical whistles erupted from all sides. Jimmy's stomach flipped over itself at the sudden speedy ascent.

"They do, Crendle! They look exactly like they did in my dream!" Krikin said.

"I'll admit, your dream-designs certainly impress even an old elf like me sometimes, Krikin," Crendle said.

"Dream designs? Dream? They look...they... They look so dangerous!" Binks added.

"Nonsense! They're almost perfectly safe!" Crendle replied.

"Al...almost?" Binks asked.

Jelly placed a steady hand on Binks elbow.

"I've been testing them all week, each one, and I signed off on their use. It just takes a little practice! That's all," Crendle said. "Why, we've only lost one elf, and Vixen is out looking for him now, so there's practically nothing to worry about!"

"Only one?" Krikin asked and smiled. "That's impressive! Better than last time at least."

"Quite right," Crendle replied.

"Wait, what? Last time?" Binks asked.

Crendle chuckled. "Fancy a go?"

"What happened last time?" Binks asked.

"Fancy a go? Do I!" Krikin said, quite ignoring Binks' question.

Binks sighed, while both Jelly and Pimsy now patted his shoulders.

Burgundy looked on and grinned, equally as eager as Krikin. Jimmy was sure that if it could, Burgundy's red hair would have glowed fiery bright, he looked so eager to fly.

The platform came to an abrupt stop just below the Bounders, causing Binks to squeak and grab one of the handrails tight.

Krikin was quick to grab one of the giant balloons. "Comfortable, too!" he said as he clamored in and situated himself within the seat. He never once seemed to take notice of how precariously high above the factory floor they now were. "Come on, everyone! They're safe, I assure you! I designed them myself."

"In your dreams? In your sleep?" Binks asked. "Dream designs?"

"Have you ever seen a better design than the ones discovered in dreams, Binks?" Krikin asked.

"Well...well no, but...."

"And have you ever known Vixen to fail in recovering an elf that tested a product?"

"No, but...."

"I'll try one!" Jimmy said.

Krikin's smile nearly split the little elf in half.

Crendle helped Jimmy into a seat and gave him a brief tutorial on the Bounders' controls. The right joystick controlled the pitch of the balloon or elevation, and the left controlled the yaw or direction.

"Just remember, right hand – up and down. Left hand – left and right. Make sense?" Crendle asked.

Jimmy nodded. "I think so!"

"Now if anything happens and ya need to come down in a hurry, just press this," Crendle said, and pointed to a small red button with a round crystal shield protecting it. "Just flip this cap open, like so, and press here. But I warn ya, it's an interesting escape to say the least! So don't press it unless ya have to! And as for this..." Crendle added, pointing to a gold button. "...this will send the Bounder back, if ya decide to end your tour somewhere else or get lost. Press the gold button, and she'll make her way home!"

"Okay! Thank you, Crendle," Jimmy said.

Crendle patted Jimmy on the shoulder and winked. "My pleasure, lad."

CHAPTER 21

THE FIRST TOY FACTORY

When everyone was strapped tight into a Bounder, Crendle pressed a glowing green button on his platform, sending it back to the factory floor amidst a cloud of bluish-white steam and wonderful whistles. Jimmy and the elves hung suspended within the Bounder corral. Everyone was laughing with anticipation. Everyone but Binks.

"I'm...I'm not sure this...this—" Binks started.

"And away ya go!" Crendle's voice said from a tiny speaker on the corral cage. Far below, the older elf pressed another button on his control panel.

"—is such a good idea," Binks finished.

Around Jimmy and the elves, the corral's sides sprung open with a loud clang, releasing the Bounders and their pilots into open air. There was a sudden jolt as the bounders found themselves loose and no longer pressed tight within the cage's confines. The sound of rubber rubbing against rubber and expanding balloons filled the air for a moment, then was replaced by tiny hums from the Bounders as their little engines whirred to life.

"Follow me, Master Jimmy!" Krikin shouted, and put his Bounder in a steep dive towards the factory floor.

Jimmy did as he was told and found the vehicle reacted to his every command, however slight. Behind him, all of the elves but one laughed, cheered, and followed suit. Binks was content to hover quietly in the corral, his eyes now shut tight.

"These are amazing, Krikin!" Pimsy shouted from her Bounder.

"Why, thank you!"

Jimmy was about to agree when Jelly sped past him, giggling as long and as hard as she was able. It was no surprise that the elf had picked a baby-blue Bounder festooned with white snowflakes. Now, with its glowing-haired pilot laughing and cheering, the craft zipped by Krikin and completed two full loops. Not to be outdone, Burgundy dove towards Jelly and spiraled over her in a beautifully executed corkscrew.

"You'll have to get one with lightning bolts painted on the sides like your skates, Burgundy!" Krikin called out after him.

"That's a wonderful idea!" Burgundy shouted back.

Jimmy was content to glide above the factory and take in all he could. The tricks the other elves were so keen to attempt could wait. After all, he was touring the first toy factory ever built! The entire workshop floor was lined with everything from massive trade tables to large woodcarving tools to tiny metalworking stations. Jimmy spotted several long pools of water and hovered close enough to watch a dozen or so elves pilot handheld model sailing ships back and forth with the aid of giant fans. When a ship would list, or worse, sink, an elf would wade out, retrieve the boat, and take it off to a station to be modified.

Beyond the pools, an enormous train set had been constructed. Jimmy flew his bounder overtop one of its tallest miniature mountains and grinned down as train after train zipped along skillfully crafted landscapes.

"Hello, Master Jimmy!" an elf called out from below. "Do you like our trains? We've been working on them all year!" he said as he held a little engine and adjusted one of its many wheels.

"Very much!" Jimmy replied.

The elf looked pleased and returned to his work. Jimmy watched as two locomotives came to a stop alongside one another and a tiny drawbridge rose up before them. Below the drawbridge, a toy sailboat, guided by wires, floated by. The entire layout must have been a thousand feet long and several hundred feet wide. Hundreds of trains, some large, some small, raced along the carefully laid tracks while elves, standing atop platforms, or crouching below, monitored their progress. Should an engine derail, it was whisked away for more adjustments, and a new engine placed in its spot. Some whistled, several puffed smoke, and a few cars were lit from within. Jimmy's father would have loved this part of the factory. He was a model train enthusiast if ever there was one. In fact, one of his first letters from Europe had eagerly described the many trains he and his fellow soldiers had seen or traveled on. The thought of his father's happier days conjured a smile, but stabbed at his heart all at the same time.

"I see you've found one of our latest toys!" a voice said from Jimmy's left. There floating next to him, in an oversized red and white Bounder, sat Santa. "These Bounders are quite fun, aren't they!"

Jimmy grinned. "Santa! Yes, they are! Very, very much!"

"I thought I would give you a tour myself, if that is all right?"

"Yes, thank you!"

"Santa! Do you like the Bounders?" Krikin asked, and swept down next to the two. He was followed by Jelly, Pimsy, and Burgundy. Binks still lingered in the corral, eyes clamped just as shut as before.

Santa chuckled. "I am very impressed, Krikin. In fact, I've been secretly zipping about on this one for the last week or so. It's quite fun indeed!"

Krikin beamed.

"Shall we continue with Jimmy's tour?" Santa asked. The elves all nodded, and off the group soared.

Jimmy was shown everything from elves manufacturing clothes to painting pictures to hand-crafting every toy imaginable. There were even elves hard at work on some of the most advanced playthings Jimmy had ever seen: tiny futuristic cars that sped about elaborate tracks without any sort of wires attached to them, and even planes and dirigibles which acted much the same way. When one of the planes zipped by Santa, he called down to an elf holding a small black box with antennae protruding from its top and congratulated him on his work. The elf nearly fell over with pride, almost crashing his tiny plane as another elf clapped him on the back.

The next area Jimmy was shown was filled with playground equipment. Tall yellow slides which spiraled over and over dotted the floor. Merry-go-rounds of every size and color spun many an elf to dizzy fits of laughter and upset stomachs. Swing-sets, see-saws, and monkey-bars were all eagerly tested by elf after elf. Jimmy noticed a dozen or more tiny fairies playing here as well; they seemed especially fond of the merry-go-rounds.

In a rather different location, hundreds of miniature dollhouses were being constructed with painstaking care for authenticity. Little yellow mansions stood next to tiny log cabins and sprawling farmhouses. Jimmy watched as several dozen elves carved the tiniest beds, desks, and rocking chairs he'd ever seen. One elf painted tiny pictures which looked no larger than postage stamps with the aid of an enormous magnifying glass. It was the only way Jimmy was able to see what exactly the elf was doing.

"You should see them make the silverware and tea-sets. It's astonishing," Santa said.

"I'll bet!" Jimmy replied.

The gift-wrapping stations were just as impressive. Hundreds of elves wrapped box after box in every color of paper imaginable. Brilliantly colored bows and ribbons were placed on present after present. When a gift was finished, it was attached to a long string, which in turn was attached to a balloon that floated skywards, where it disappeared.

"Would you like to see where they go?" Santa asked as Jimmy watched one of the presents float away.

"Yes, please!"

"Then up we go!" Santa said, soaring high into the air.

Jimmy followed and marveled as the floor faded completely from sight. When he thought they could travel no higher, a floating ocean of wrapped presents came into view above. Santa guided his Bounder up through the present-adorned ceiling and disappeared. Jimmy followed and gasped as he broke through the surface of boxes. Millions of colored balloons were being funneled through a large opening even higher above.

"This is where we send the presents now. It's far more efficient than the old assembly line tracks we used to use," Santa said. "Plus, it allows for far more floor space."

Jimmy stared about. "Wow."

A moment later, the elves emerged through the sea of presents and made their way over to Santa and Jimmy.

"Care to see where they go from here?" Santa asked.

Jimmy looked up to the tunnel where the balloons were headed and grinned. "Can we?"

"Of course! Stay close now."

Santa flew onward. As they grew closer, Jimmy noticed the tunnel was created by the tree's very roots. In fact, the root system itself was busy guiding the balloons through the opening and untangling any bunched or twisted presents. Santa, Jimmy, and the elves made their way amongst the floating gifts and were soon surrounded by the brightly wrapped packages. After a while, the tunnel leveled off, and the busy roots faded behind them. Here the walls were smooth and brightly polished, almost glasslike. Giant fans began to dot the tunnels walls, ceiling and floor. As the bounders drifted by, Jimmy could feel the fans blowing them and the stream of presents along. Right from the outset, elves reached out from various windows and pulled gift after gift from the flow. Several waved and cheered as the troupe drifted by.

"Neat!" Jimmy said.

Santa chuckled, the elves laughed, and poor Binks waited back in the corral.

CHAPTER 22

KRIKIN'S HOME

When they reached the end of the tunnel, only a single floating present remained. Jimmy stared at the lone small box. It was unlike any of the other gifts which had floated by, as the wrapping and bow alike were shades of darkest black and coldest shadow. The sight of the little present sent a cold, prickly chill up Jimmy's spine. Santa flew his Bounder to a nearby balcony and dismounted. Jimmy and the elves followed suit.

"I especially like this part," Santa said to Krikin. He reached over to his Bounder and pressed the gold button. The Bounder whirred to life, hovered about on its own, twisted in the air once, and sped back down the tunnel towards its home.

"Crendle liked that, too," Krikin said, and pressed his own golden button.

Jimmy and the elves did the same and watched their empty Bounders spring to life and disappear.

"Did we forget poor Binks?" Santa asked.

Jelly and Pimsy gasped. Burgundy and Krikin chuckled.

"I think he was just a little, tiny bit nervous about the Bounders," Krikin said.

Santa looked surprised. "Binks, afraid of heights? Interesting." He snapped his fingers. There was a shower of gold glitter, several small pops, and Binks appeared.

The little elf opened one eye, took a deep breath, and opened the other. He smiled and sighed with obvious relief. "Whew! Thank you, thank you, thank you!" the elf said, and dusted off a bit of the shimmering flakes.

"Since when have you ever been afraid of heights, Binks?" Santa asked.

"You know, I'm... I'm not really too sure! No offense to Krikin and his designs, I just, I... I can't explain it! I was just scared, and I can't tell you why, Santa. I'm sorry, and I'm sorry Krikin, I really wanted to try your invention, I truly did. Maybe it was because the Bounders were new to me? I have no other excuse."

Krikin and Santa comforted Binks, reassuring him that everything was okay while apologizing for leaving him behind. Binks seemed unfazed by the unintentional slight and more relieved at being back on the ground than anything else.

Santa patted Binks on the head and turned to the group. "Well, you will have to forgive me, but I must be going again. And speaking of leaving...would you all like to accompany me tonight? I have been forced to move Alexander's trip forward a bit, and I'm sure he would enjoy the companionship."

"Do you think he will want to remain there, Santa? I mean, if this truly is Alexander's old home?" Krikin asked.

"I'm not entirely sure, Krikin. Remember, Alexander has been searching for his past for a very, very long time."

Krikin looked down at his feet and sighed. "I just...I guess I'll just miss him if he decides to stay."

"We all will, Krikin. But what kind of friends would we be if we asked dear old Alexander to give up a chance to learn where he came from, or find his family again?"

The elf nodded. "He did seem excited at the news, didn't he?"

Santa nodded. "He most certainly did."

"I'll miss him too, Krikin," Pimsy said. "But at least we can visit him now and then, remember."

Burgundy stepped forward and placed his hand on Krikin's shoulder. "I think we would all be honored to accompany Alexander home, Santa. I mean, who better to send him off than his friends?"

Everyone agreed.

"In the meantime, we have much more to show Master Jimmy, let's not forget!" Jelly said.

"I will leave you to it then," Santa replied. He then retrieved the strange black present, snapped his fingers, and vanished in a shower of gold, red and green light.

"He's so... so good at that!" Binks said. "I can barely pop from one room to the next without getting stuck in a wall or door half the time."

The elves chuckled, and the mood improved.

Krikin turned to Jimmy. "Since we're already here, would you like to see my home?"

"Yes, please!" Jimmy said. The idea of seeing how an elf lived when not at work or play was intriguing.

Krikin led the group through a large door, and they found themselves in the same lobby of elevator shafts as before. Krikin located a tube labeled 'Homes' and pressed a small green button in the shape of a Christmas tree. Jimmy and the elves stared skyward and watched the elevators run about in an endless ballet of wood and brass. For a second Jimmy thought he saw one of the shafts change direction but couldn't be certain. A minute later their elevator arrived, and several elves exited.

"This is a fun trip!" Krikin said. When everyone was inside, he pressed a button labeled "K" and the cart shot skyward.

The speed at which the elevator raced was impressive. Not only that, but it began to twist and turn through shafts which made long arcs left, right and back, over and over again. By the time the elevator stopped, everyone was laughing.

"That is a fun route!" Burgundy said, and stepped out.

Jelly nodded. "I think that was even faster than last weeks'."

"The elevators change routes from time to time," Krikin explained. "I think they like to surprise us every now and then. You know, throw us for a loop when they can."

"Literally!" Binks said. "Remember the trip to B-Level last month? Those loopty-loops had me spinning and spinning and spinning for ages after a ride home."

"Oh yes! Those *were* fun," Jelly agreed.

"I think the ride to S-Level has a loop or two in it now," Binks said. "I've been too scared to find out. I can still feel those trips when I close my eyes at night."

Jimmy and the elves chuckled and followed Krikin down a cozy hallway lined with hundreds of doorways. Every few feet, a small hearth burned in an effort to keep the passageway warm and lit. Oval carpets dotted the hallway, their colors rotating from green to red to gold and back again for the entire length. Small chairs and tables were stationed every so often, and each contained either a chess table or stack of books. When Krikin found his door, he twisted a silver knob and ushered everyone inside.

"Welcome!" he said, and followed the last person in.

Krikin's home was warm and friendly. The first room was the main living space. It was lined with comfy-looking chairs, a long couch and a large fireplace, which burned bright as if expecting them. Not one, but two Christmas trees stood on either side of the hearth.

"Krikin, this is wonderful!" Pimsy said.

"It is!" Jelly agreed. "I can't wait for my turn in the Tree next year."

"Why, thank you!" Krikin replied. "It's nowhere near as large as the homes outside, but what does size matter for an elf?"

A giggle rippled through the friends, and Krikin began taking coats, hats and scarves. When everyone had cups of cocoa, cookies, and various other refreshments, Krikin gave a small tour of his tiny abode. Beyond the living room sat a petite dining area which allowed for several guests to be seated comfortably. The table here appeared to have been grown right out of the floor and was flanked on three sides by large windows overlooking the great forest far below. The kitchen was next, and Jimmy noticed that Krikin had not one, not two, but three stoves installed in various locations. He was a Silver-Belled Chef after all, Jimmy thought. There was also a second fireplace here; though similar to its cousin in the living room, it was taller and several feet deeper. It also contained a large, cast-iron cooking apparatus, and a small fire within the hearth was busy cooking something that smelled of apples and cinnamon inside a suspended dutch oven. All along the kitchen's ceiling hung various dried herbs, flowers, and fruits, whose aromas mingled about the home in a plethora of pleasantly pungent perfumes. The countertops which were spotless simply sparkled; nary a crumb, nor fleck of flour could be noted here. The counters, too, appeared to have grown right out of the walls and floor, with many a neat cupboard below. The kitchen radiated a well-used and equally well-loved atmosphere.

After the kitchen and dining room, Krikin showed everyone to his garden, which they entered by means of the living room and two French doors. Three wooden steps lead down to the garden which stood within a polished glass greenhouse. It jutted out beyond the walls of the First Tree to accommodate a beautiful glass ceiling. Even the floor was glass, which took Jimmy by surprise at first. Then he remembered how sturdy the staircase that Santa had summoned in the travel lodge had been, and he sighed in relief.

The garden was lit with orbs of light which hovered about in lazy bobs and shallow sways. It smelled wonderful. There were various herbs, a strawberry patch, a blueberry bush, a tiny orange tree, two apple trees, a pumpkin patch, and more vegetables than Jimmy could count. Outside, snow had begun to fall again, and the roof of the greenhouse began to dust over in flakes.

"I spend a lot of time down here," Krikin said, and plucked a lemon from a nearby tree.

"You do so well with the fruits," Jelly said. "I always have a hard time with them in the winter."

"It's the fairy lights," Krikin replied, and nodded to one of the floating orbs. "This time of year you need a few extra. I've also found that a little music never hurts."

Jelly cocked her head to the side. "Music? I never thought of that, but I'll try it!"

"They especially like Master Bing," Krikin added.

"Who doesn't?" Binks agreed.

Burgundy and Pimsy strolled up and down the garden aisles, stopping every few feet to admire a flower here, a fruit there.

"How long do you get to live here, Krikin?" Jimmy asked.

"Each elf gets a year at a time in the tree. The larger the tree has gotten, the fewer years one has to wait. This is my first time actually, but Crendle says I may only have to wait a couple more before I can come back, and someday, the hope is that anyone who wishes can live here all the time!"

"That would be fun," Jimmy said. He was reminded of his current place of address, certainly not his home, and wished he hadn't been. His heart sank, and he tried to push the image of the children's ward from his mind. It was difficult.

"Oh, it is fun! Fun indeed," Krikin replied.

Jimmy forced a smile and wondered if the elves could see the effort behind it.

For the next hour, Jimmy and his new friends rested in Krikin's living room. They chatted about everything from dragons to reindeer to favorite fudge recipes. More cocoa and cider was poured, more cookies were eaten, and more smiles appeared. Krikin and Burgundy baked up a loaf of savory-smelling bread on which they melted a pungent and aromatic cheese. Jimmy tried to remember some of the lyrics the two sang for the recipes. They were entertaining verses, and cheerful. Jelly opened Krikin's radio cabinet, fiddled with the nobs and found Bing Crosby singing to the troops on the Armed Forces Network. His voice was soft and pleasant. Jelly sang along.

"I'm dreaming of a white Christmas,
just like the ones I used to know.
Where the treetops glisten,
and children listen
To hear sleigh bells in the snow."

"I think 'White Christmas' must be the loveliest and saddest song ever written," Jelly said.

"My mother loves this song, but she cries when it's played," Jimmy said. "It reminds her of my dad and my uncle."

The elves all looked to one another and bowed their heads.

"I remember your uncle, Master Freddy, quite well," Krikin said, his voice trembled low.

"You met my uncle?" Jimmy asked.

"Well, we never met face-to-face like you and I, but I helped make several of the toys he wrote Santa about when he was young," Krikin said. A salty tear leapt from his cheek and plunged into his sweet cocoa. "I carved two planes for him, in fact, and a yo-yo! I even helped put a decoration or two on his tree as his parents couldn't afford many that year...the Great Depression and all that."

"That was nice of you, Krikin," Jimmy said.

The elf looked up, and he too forced a smile.

"Should we maybe... move on, perhaps?" Burgundy suggested. "If we're to send Alexander off today, we should put away these sad thoughts, yes? Lighten the mood a bit?" he said, and winked a not-so-sly wink to the elves.

Broad smiles returned then, and thoughts of war and the inevitable tragedies that accompany it drifted away.

CHAPTER 23

SOARING SPIRITS

E veryone helped clean Krikin's dirty dishes, donned their coats, caps, and scarves, and headed off towards the elevators again.

Krikin pressed a button to call their ride and patted Jimmy on the shoulder. "You will loooooooooove this part!"

"This is my most favorite thing ever I think…even more than snow skating, I do believe!" Jelly said.

Jimmy grinned at the elf, whose hair blazed brighter and brighter the longer they waited. When the car arrived, everyone stepped in, and Krikin pressed a green button simply labeled "Top".

"I dunno why this doesn't bother me…." Binks said as the cart raced higher and higher.

"That is strange," Krikin replied. "Considering the…." he stopped, glanced at Jimmy, and grinned. "Never mind," he added with a sly nod to the other elves.

Jimmy wasn't sure what his friends were discussing, or rather trying not to discuss, but he knew that whatever it was it must involve very high places considering how long they'd been traveling now. The elevator continued its journey up and up and up for what seemed an eternity until at last the cart came to a stop. The doors opened onto a long narrow hallway lined with tiny frosted windows.

"It doesn't feel too windy!" Pimsy said.

"I kind of like the windy rides...erm...." Burgundy stopped himself before divulging anymore of the surprise.

The elves led Jimmy down the hallway, stopping occasionally to peer out of one of the unclouded windows. As far as Jimmy could tell, they were near the very top of the First Tree, for as hard as he tried he could barely make out the tops of the clouds far below. Not only that, but the stars above shined through the small amount of daylight as bright and as clear as they had when he'd seen them from Santa's sleigh at night. The further the group walked, the smaller the hallway became, and the more Jimmy was sure he could feel the entire thing swaying to and fro beneath his feet.

"Here we are!" Krikin said, pausing before a tiny wooden door painted green and blue. "Now stay close, Master Jimmy! And hold the railing tight!"

Krikin opened the door, and a torrent of frosty air burst into the little hallway. One by one, the group stepped outside onto the very edge of one of the highest branches. The air here was as clean and crisp as Jimmy had ever smelled. A minuscule wooden railing was all that stood between anyone on the limb and an endless fall to the forest floor far, far below.

"Whoa!" Jimmy said. He could not stop himself from smiling.

"Whoa is right!" Burgundy replied.

"Come on lads and lasses!" a busy-sounding voice called out from further down the branch. "I'm about to send off the last few here, so time is of the essence! How many, six? Just enough! Let's go, let's go, let's go!"

Jimmy spotted the source of the voice and followed the group towards a brightly-dressed elf holding a large leaf in one hand and gripping the railing before him with the other. Trip appeared older than the other elves, had yellow and purple hair, a tiny beard, and bright purple eyes. His hat and coat were both red with spiraling white stripes. Along each white band were tiny green leaf designs, and his boots were covered in what looked to be brown and gold tree bark. As Jimmy looked closer, he saw the bark making up Trip's boots was alive and holding him to the branch in a steadfast and sturdy grip.

"Hello, Trip!" Krikin said. "We've brought along Master Jimmy!"

Trip cocked his head to get a better look at Jimmy, who was near the end of the line, and grinned. "Brought him to the best ride in the park, did ya?"

"I think so, yes!" Krikin said.

"Oh, it is, it is!" Jelly agreed.

"It's a pleasure to meet ya, lad!" Trip said. "I'm the flight controller on this section of the ol' tree! Ready for a go?" Trip's purple eyes twinkled.

"I umm…." Jimmy said. "I don't know? Am I?"

Trip and the rest of the elves laughed.

"You'll be all right lad, I promise! I haven't lost a rider yet this season!" Trip said.

"Just watch me, Master Jimmy, and do what I do!" Jelly said, as she worked her way to the front of the line.

"Good to see you again, Jelly," Trip said, and handed her an enormous emerald leaf, its edges gilded in shiny silver.

Trip reached down to the railing and retrieved a small brown bag which was tied there. He opened the pouch, reached in, and sprinkled some of its contents over the beautiful leaf, which Jelly now held wide. A shower of blue and orange flakes covered the foliage, and Jelly's smile widened.

"I think that should do it!" Trip said. "Now mind the cross-winds above the forest, and you'll be fine!"

Trip let the bag drop, dusted off his hands, and unlatched a small section of railing before them. Jelly's hair turned a bright shade of baby-blue, and off she leapt, holding the leaf close to her chest.

"WHOA!" Jimmy shouted as his friend began zipping about below them.

The leaf carried the elf with little effort and glided wherever she wished with just the slightest of movements.

"You said it, lad!" Trip agreed, and waved as Jelly zipped off, laughing and giggling the entire time.

"Ready for a go, Master Jimmy?" Krikin asked.

"Yes, please!"

Trip walked a short way down the branch and reached into a crate full of various leaves. As he did, Jimmy noticed the elf's boots would release and refasten themselves to the branch with every step.

"This one should do ya nicely!" Trip said. He handed Jimmy a larger emerald leaf and sprinkled his magic glitter over its surface. Jimmy felt the leaf vibrate in his hands, and it begin to emit a soft, pleasant hum. The silver which lined the leafs edges grew warm, which Jimmy was thankful for, as his hands were beginning to get a little cold this far up.

"Mind your grip. Ya don' have to strangle her now. She won't let ya fall, I promise," Trip said. "All ya have to do is tilt yourself in any direction ya like, and she'll glide wherever ya want."

"Thank you," Jimmy replied. "And it was nice meeting you!"

Trip opened the gate. "The pleasure was mine, lad."

"I'll be right behind you, Master Jimmy! Just follow Jelly and she'll lead us down," Krikin said.

Jimmy took a deep breath, held the leaf tight to his chest and leapt out into the void. The leaf did exactly as Trip promised and carried him out over the silver clouds below as if he were simply a feather on the back of a warm summer breeze.

"YAHOO!!!" Jimmy yelled. Behind him he heard Trip, Krikin, and the rest cheer him on.

"Master Jimmy! Over here!" Jelly shouted from just below.

Jimmy leaned towards the elf, and the leaf soared down as instructed.

"Was I right? Or was I really, really, really right?" Jelly asked as Jimmy swooped past her in a long, carefully executed spiral.

"I feel like the luckiest bird in the world!" Jimmy said.

Jelly laughed and raced next to Jimmy's side. "Here they come!" she said, and just above, Krikin, Burgundy, Pimsy, and Binks soared towards them. Trip waved and cheered from the branch.

The elves swooped and soared over the forest for quite some time. The wind picked up a bit as they neared the forest's canopy, but it only offered Burgundy and Krikin another chance to try and outdo one another in aerial acrobatics. When the group landed, Jimmy barely felt the snow beneath him. Like a feather landing on a bed of more feathers and cotton balls, he thought.

"What did you think of that?" Pimsy asked.

"You were right! That was very, very fun!"

"I daresay even more exciting than my Bounders!" Krikin replied.

"I'll second and third and fourth that!" Binks agreed.

When everyone was situated, the leaves took flight again and returned to the Tree to continue their jobs ferrying elves to and fro.

CHAPTER 24

TREASURE SEEKERS

"I think we still have time for one more stop if you would like, Master Jimmy?" Krikin asked.

"Sure! Although I don't know how you could top that!" Everyone laughed.

"Well, I'm not sure either, but I think you might like this anyway," Krikin said. "Have you ever seen a candy mine?"

"A what?"

Krikin grinned. "No? Good!"

"That's a great idea, Krikin!" Jelly said. "I've been meaning to gather a few things for the Claus kitchen anyway."

"That too is a great idea, Pimsy," Binks said. "I've been running low on cotton candy crystals with all of the sugar clouds Mrs. Claus has us practicing!"

"A candy mine?" Jimmy asked.

"Oh yes, you'll love it!" Jelly replied. "And we can pick up something for Alexander while we're there. A nice selection of sweets as a going-away present!"

Everyone whistled for their snow skates, which soon raced into sight. Burgundy was the first to have his fastened, and he shooed

141

his boots away. The boots did as they were told, and the red-haired elf began skating circles around the group.

"I remember the first time I ever saw the mines!" Burgundy mused. "Nicodemus had to chase me out of there so many times, I figured he'd tell Santa to outright forbid me to go anywhere near 'em again!"

Krikin nodded, sent his boots home and began skating after Burgundy. "I remember taking Dasher when he was finally old enough. I hear he works there whenever he's able to these days."

"Dasher helps in the mines?" Pimsy asked. "Is there anything that boy doesn't do?"

"He does! I hear he's not fond of staying still for too long," Binks joked.

Soon everyone had their snow skates fastened and their boots flying off to get warm and dry again. Krikin led the group back into the forest, making several detours along the way to point out various sites of interest to Jimmy. They passed a flower farm where everything from roses to petunias bloomed by the thousands. It seemed the cold was no match for the elves' green thumbs and fairy lights. There was an enormous field of ice sculptures where figures of animals, toys, and more were all carved from crystal-clear ice and lit from within by tiny colored lights. Elves old and young strolled through the displays, marveling at the intricate designs and brilliant colors. They even passed by a miniature village of houses where hundreds of tiny mice decorated minuscule trees in their tiny yards or built itty-bitty snowmen with their children.

"I'm still going to miss Alexander," Krikin said as they passed the mice and their village.

"We all will, Krikin," Jelly reassured him.

"I wonder... I wonder if Nix... You know... I wonder if Nix knows? They were such, such good friends and all," Binks said. "I just... I don't think... I..."

Jelly glided over to Binks and took his hand in hers, and he immediately relaxed. They skated along like that for a ways.

"Oh, I'm sure Nix knows, Binks," Krikin replied. "They're probably visiting one another now."

"Nix is the snow-person you mentioned earlier, right?" Jimmy asked.

"The very one," Binks replied. "He's lived here longer than just about anyone, though he travels quite a bit; always following winter around the world."

"And he's made of snow?"

"He sure is!" Burgundy said. "I love the snow people. They're always so very happy. And boy can they sled!"

"Nix lets me ride on his back when we go sledding sometimes!" Pimsy said. "He's soooooooo fast! Faster than even the flitter-leaves!"

"Flitter-leaves?" Jimmy asked.

"That's what we call the leaves that we just flew around on," Pimsy said. "Flitter-leaves!"

"Ahh."

It wasn't long before a steep gray and white mountain appeared above the trees like a frozen wave of ice and rock. As they skated closer, Jimmy spotted tiny carts racing up and down the nearest slopes atop what appeared to be a network of glowing railroad tracks. Some carts had elves nestled within, others carried mounds of what looked to be ice, while several more pulsed with mysterious blue and gold lights. The forest came to a scattered end just at the base of the mountain, and Krikin led the group towards a large stone building surrounded by dwarves—or at least that's what Jimmy assumed. They certainly looked like he'd imagined a dwarf would look, and they were clearly of different build and stature than the elves and fairies he'd met today. Not to mention their lengthy beards one and all.

The building they approached was nearly four stories tall on one end, with a roof which sloped away from the mountain and stopped quite close to the snow-covered ground on the opposite end. It looked to Jimmy like a giant ramp. Long steel cables, as thick as Jimmy's arms, stretched out of the tallest side of the building and disappeared into the clouds high up the slopes. The front of the building facing the mountain was wide open to the elements, and the stones which made up the building's three primary walls were of various size, shape and color; no two appeared alike, though they fit snug next to and atop one another as if they'd been formed that way. In fact, the stones fit together so well, there didn't even appear for a need of grout to keep them there. It was marvelous construction. Even the building's roof was made of stone. Several large windows pulsed brightly from an unseen source of light within, and thunderous clangs, jarring pings, and shuddering bangs occasionally echoed out of the stone structure.

Krikin skated up to a burly-looking dwarf with a lengthy blonde beard standing just outside. He was smoking a long ebony pipe which issued forth pink and purple smoke; it smelled like spiced berries and vanilla.

"Good day, Master Niping!" Krikin said, bowing.

The dwarf turned, lowered his pipe, tipped his cap, and bowed in return. "Young Krikinfield."

Krikin motioned at Jimmy and the elves. "I was wondering if you might allow us to take Master Jim on a tour of the mines? He's never been in a mine before, much less a candy mine!"

Niping looked at Jimmy and studied him for a moment. "So this is the lad everyone's been talking about."

"Hello, sir," Jimmy replied.

Niping nodded, tipped his cap, and turned his attention back to Krikin. "Ya understand what week it is, Krikinfield? What with Christmas 'round the corner 'n all. It's hectic in the mines, lad," Niping said. He took a deep breath, sighed, took another draw from his pipe, sighed again, and looked back at Jimmy and the rest of the elves. After a moment, he shook his head and chuckled. "Let us see what Tagish has to say 'bout tours at present."

Niping reached for a small pocket on the front of his jacket. He withdrew a pearl-colored whistle and gave three quick blows. Seconds later a stunning silver hawk swooped down and landed on the dwarf's outstretched arm. The bird leaned close to Niping's ear, chirped once, and Niping whispered something in return. The hawk nodded and raced back into the sky towards the mountain.

"Be quick and there's an extra treat fer ya when ya return!" Niping shouted up. The hawk called back in reply.

"Thank you!" Krikin said.

"Not at all, lad, but Fenrin may be a while. Ol' Tagish is deep in the southern tunnels last I heard. Let's go 'round to the fires 'till she returns."

The dwarf led Jimmy and the elves behind the building, where dozens of tiny fires burned, each surrounded by dwarves and elves alike. Some melted blocks of cheese or roasted potatoes over the flames, while others sported sleeve-length metal gloves that shined bright gold and copper. Those who wore these metal gauntlets held equally beautiful steins right in the blazing flames, heating whatever beverage they were enjoying. The smell of chestnuts, coffee, tea, chocolate, and numerous other delights swirled around the busy camp. Near one corner of the building, half a dozen polar bears stood around a large berry bush, grazing away, the fur around their mouths stained purple and blue. Jimmy noticed they all wore saddles and harnesses.

Niping followed Jimmy's stare. "Ya need to keep 'em full of their favorite berries, or they'll devour half o' the candy we mine when they're in the tunnels," he said. "Some of the elves came up with the idea to grow many-berry-bushes, which keeps 'em satisfied most o' the time. Nice little feat o' horticultural engineerin' if ya ask me. I've seen as many as two dozen different types o' fruit on that there plant, all at once mind ya! And quite a few o' the fruits are a strange combination of several other fruits all mixed into one!"

"Wow," Jimmy replied.

"I've been trying to grow orange and lime berries for ages now," Jelly said. "I keep getting these little purple ones that taste like apples!"

Krikin laughed. "I can help you with that."

"So you've never been to a mine?" Niping asked.

Jimmy tore his eyes away from the giant fruit-stained bears and glanced about. "No, sir, not like this. Actually, I've ever seen a mine of any kind."

Niping shook his head. "That's a shame, lad; I hope Tagish lets ya see a bit today. In the meantime, if ya look up, you'll notice we've built a nice tram o' sorts for the heavier loads comin' down from the mountain. The first dwarves to come here brought what rare metals they had an' spun those cables using the ancient methods. They're stronger than steel an' lighter than my beard! We've never had one break, and believe me when I tell ya, we've certainly tried."

Just then a long white and gold cart glided down one of the cables. It slowed near the bottom and disappeared into the stone building.

Niping sniffed the air at its passing. "Still no peppermint this season. That smells like more butterscotch."

"So, the mines…I mean, you mine candy? They're full of candy?" Jimmy asked.

Niping grinned. "Candy the likes ya can't imagine, lad. Candy so rare that only a handful has ever left the North Pole. Crystals so pure an' so magnificent we couldn't bring ourselves to cut 'em. I've seen wonders within these mountains that would leave even a dragon speechless, an' that's sayin' somethin'!"

"So you don't mine for gold, or silver, or...I don't know...gems and minerals?" Jimmy asked.

Niping laughed, his great yellow beard bouncing about. "Oh, we mine for those as well. But if ya ask me lad, no gold glitters as much, nor gem glimmers as bright, as a child's smile when given somethin' sweet. That's why we mine here. Ya can't put a price on a child's happiness, after all. That, and there's nothin' better at helping someone remember their youth than with a taste or flavor they loved as a child. And what child doesn't love candy? It's far easier to share such gifts than, say, a bag o' pretty diamonds, which don't really do anything more than sparkle. After all, I've never seen a war fought over candy canes and bubble gum! But don't get me started on all of that, we'll be here 'till next Christmas."

"I... I think you do a wonderfully, wonderful job here, Niping," Binks said. "I'll never ever forget my first trip through the mines. Santa took me himself. That was the first time I saw cherry crystals, and a vanilla river!"

Niping tipped his hat and re-lit his pipe. "Then I hope ya get to see our new find, young Binkrindrican. We just discovered the source o' the white river last week. And to say it's a sight to behold would be a grand understatement indeed."

Another cart glided down the mountain as the first one raced back out of the building towards the mines high above. Niping sniffed the air, his mouth fell open, and his eyes grew wide. Before he could say anything, faint but hearty cheers could be heard coming from inside the cart as it descended.

"Sounds like they found something!" Burgundy said.

"Somethin' is right, lad! An' from the smell of it, they found a rare somethin'!" Niping replied.

"Is that Master Nicodemus with them?" Krikin asked.

Everyone stared as best they could at the cart racing down the mountainside. As it drew closer, the dwarves and elves standing about the fires raced towards the landing area and began to cheer.

147

"I think I see Fenrin," Jimmy said.

"That's him circlin' the load alright. If what I think is in the hold, then Tagish's in there with it," Niping replied.

A minute later the great cart came to rest at the base of the mountain. Everyone raced over and stared up, eager to see what had been unearthed. There was an agonizing moment of stillness from the cart, and then a giant, furry white figure climbed into view. Jimmy took a step back and his heart began to race, for the giant standing within the cart looked anything but friendly.

"Tagish! Tagish! Tagish!" the crowd cheered.

Jimmy relaxed when he saw a small round man with long red beard, red cap, and blue earmuffs sitting astride the giant's shoulder.

"We've found it!" the man shouted over the crowd. "One hundred and eleven years since we've seen this, and now Santa can take the legendary Royal Peppermint to the children of the world again!"

The shouts and cheers that exploded from the growing crowd sent goosebumps racing across Jimmy's arms. Whatever this Royal Peppermint was, it was an undoubtedly exciting find.

"And this time, my friends... this time, there looks to be enough for everyone!"

Krikin elbowed Jimmy and shouted over the crowd. "Last time, there wasn't enough for anyone at the North Pole! We gave it all to the children. This will be the first time many of us have ever had a chance to try Royal Peppermint!"

"What's Royal Peppermint?" Jimmy shouted back.

Though he thought only Krikin could hear him, the entire crowd of dwarves and elves fell suddenly silent.

"Who said that?" Nicodemus asked. He began to laugh. "Was that this Jim-boy I've been hearin' about?"

Jimmy's face flushed. "Yes, sir."

Everyone turned to face Jimmy and his friends.

"What's Royal Peppermint, indeed! Well, come on up and take a gander, boy! See for yourself!" Nicodemus said.

The crowd parted, and Jimmy skated towards the cart, his heart racing. When he was just below the tram, Nicodemus whispered something into the giant creature's ear, and suddenly Jimmy found himself in one of the beast's hands being lifted up into the air in one smooth, gentle motion. Before he could say thank you, his eyes fell upon the cart's payload, and his jaw dropped.

"Tagish, Tagish Nicodemus at your service!" The man said. "Pretty, isn't it?"

Jimmy was at a loss. After everything he'd seen, after all the times he was left speechless, it still stunned him to find that he was unable to comment on something. Yet here he was again, without words to describe his feelings. The entire cart's bed was filled with what looked like boulders of colored glass, all the size of Jimmy or larger. Each stone was so perfectly clear that you could see right through it, and reddish-purple veins ran through each. The scent was breathtaking.

"THAT, my boy, is Royal Peppermint!" Nicodemus said.

"Wow," Jimmy replied.

"Wow indeed!" Nicodemus said.

The crowd cheered again, and hats flew into the air.

CHAPTER 25

WHAT'S MINED IS YOURS

When everyone managed to calm down, Nicodemus ordered the cart unloaded, and Jimmy was placed on the strange creature's opposite shoulder. He was surprised to find how soft the brilliant white fur was, not to mention warm. The tram lurched forward again and glided into the stone building.

"This here's Grumble! He's a yeti, but don't let that fool ya! He's a downright friendly lump o' fur, aren't ya, Grumby!" Nicodemus said, tugging at the yeti's fur. "Fenrin tells me you lot would like a tour o' the mines?"

Jimmy tore his eyes from the goings-on around him and found his voice again. "Yes, sir, if that would be alright."

Nicodemus laughed. "Well, normally this time of year I'd say no, but seeing how we just struck a vein of this here Royal, I couldn't possible deny you a gander now, could I?"

"Ummm...."

"Niping!" Nicodemus shouted towards the group. "Go on and have a travel-cart loaded onto the South tracks, please. I'll be there directly."

Niping grinned, tipped his cap, and began giving orders to get the new cart ready.

"And Fenrin!" Nicodemus said. "Go tell Santa the good news if you would, please!"

Fenrin chirped, leapt from the rafters, and soared out of the building to deliver the message.

All about the cart, dwarves and elves worked at long stone tables sorting every imaginable color of candy. Before Jimmy was able to see more, the yeti reached down, unlocked the cart's giant doors, and leapt to the floor. As soon as he did, half a dozen elves began carrying the Royal Peppermint off into the workshop with the help of large red and green wagons.

"Let's go outside, Grumby!" Nicodemus said.

The giant lumbered across the workspace and stepped through a large door at the rear. High up on the mountain, a bright display of purple fireworks was being set off to cheers and whistles all over the camp.

"We let loose with the fireworks whenever we find somethin' rare. I dare say we'll attract a crowd now fer sure! It's been many an age since the Purples burst overhead," Nicodemus explained.

Grumble set Jimmy and Nicodemus down and trudged off towards the many-berry-bush to share a snack with the bears. His footsteps shook the ground as he left.

"Congratulations, Nic," a voice said.

Jimmy and Nicodemus turned to see Niping on his way back.

"Thank ya kindly, Nip."

Niping nodded and motioned to the elves that stood grinning over his shoulder. "A travel-cart is being prepped for this lot as we speak. I appreciate you allowing them to tour the mine when we're so close to Christmas."

Nicodemus smiled. "Of course, but you'll have to take 'em yourself, Nip. I've loads of work to oversee and nowhere near 'nuff time to see it done."

Niping tipped his hat and patted Nicodemus on the shoulder. "I'll return and help soon enough. It's a wonder you weren't born a dwarf, Nic. I'm still convinced there's some trace of Dwarven blood in those veins of yours; they run far too deep to be anything else."

Nicodemus blushed. "Mighty nice of ya to say so, Nip."

Jimmy thought he saw the little round man wipe away a tear while turning his head to disguise the motion.

There was an awkward pause, and Nicodemus cleared his throat. "Now you lot don't dilly-dally up there too long! And don't you go gittin' yourself lost again, Miss Jelly!"

"Oh I won't, Master Nicodemus, I promise!" the little elf replied.

"Good, good. Well, I'm off; it was nice to meet ya, Jim. Oh, and before I forget, you lot take these with ya," Nicodemus dug into his coat. He retrieved half a dozen white sacks and handed them to Krikin. "They hold more than they look like they do, larger on the inside 'n all that. Take what ya can carry, and that goes fer yer bellies if ya like!"

Everyone thanked the little round man again and followed Niping towards a smaller cart waiting to carry them up the slopes. Jimmy took note of several dozen giant leaves gliding overhead, no doubt carrying elves to investigate the reason for these legendary purple fireworks.

"Master Niping," Binks said. "When... When you mentioned Master Nicodemus's ancestry, the idea that Dwarven blood should run in his veins, he seemed, well, he seemed a little sad."

Niping turned towards the tiny elf and nodded. "Nicodemus never knew his parents, young Binkrindrican. He came to the North Pole many an age ago, after searching the world for 'em. A long while passed when he wouldn't admit what it was he was actually looking for. Silver and gold, he'd say, silver and gold. But Santa knew better, and some of the elves had their doubts as well.

It took time, but eventually Nicodemus told his tale, and Santa tried his best to help find his long lost parents. When Santa himself was unable to locate them, he offered Nicodemus a home here in the North, and he's been here ever since."

"That's so very, very sad!" Pimsy said.

"Aye, lass, but ol' Nic has a new family now, and I like to think he's at peace," the dwarf replied. "Remember, friends are simply the family you pick for yourself. And they are just as important and love you no less than you should be."

"That's a wonderful way of looking at it," Krikin said.

Niping winked. "Because it's true, lad."

When they reached the travel-cart, Jimmy and the elves called for their boots and sent their snow skates off to rest and get warm. Niping opened one of the two doors, and everyone piled in. Jimmy and Niping placed Krikin between them, and on the other side of the cart, Pimsy, Burgundy, Jelly, and Binks squeezed onto the second seat. Niping then pressed a series of glowing buttons near the side of the car, and several whistles sounded from somewhere further up the mountain.

"Now make sure ya wear these," Niping said. He reached below his seat and produced a brightly colored hard-hat, which he placed atop his head. "Ya never know what the mountains might do, even the friendly ones." The elves followed suit.

"Friendly ones?" Jimmy asked as he adjusted his red and purple hat.

"Aye, lad. Mountains have souls, and with a soul comes a disposition, a temperament if you will. Some souls are mischievous by nature, some kind, and some...well, some are not," Niping said. "Either way, it's best to approach them with the proper respect. Not to mention, noggin protection," he finished, rapping his knuckles on the top of his hat.

The rest of the elves replaced their caps with hardhats and settled in for the long ride up the mountain. Niping closed the door and pulled a lever on the opposite side of the cart. There was a moment's pause, a small vibration, and off they went, pulled along by an unseen force. The cart rolled along without so much as a bump, gradually gaining in speed.

"Looks like snow further up," Krikin said, pointing to large gray clouds settling over the highest peaks.

"Aye, smells like several feet are in store fer us," Niping replied. "Best to huddle close, and mind yer feet," he said, tapping the floor of the cart with his long pipe. A small panel popped open, and a glowing orange crystal rose into the cart. Niping blew a tiny amount of smoke onto the gem, and it began to shine even brighter. It didn't take long for the entire cart to fill with warmth.

"Neat!" Jimmy said.

Niping chuckled. "The elves aren't the only ones with a touch o' magic behind their beards, or up their sleeves, lad. That's dragon obsidian. It's molten glass created by dragon fire, and it never truly cools. All one has to do is expose it to a little smoke, and there ya go! You've got yerself a nice little heater! Krymson makes these fer us, as does Vellrex from time to time. Krymson tends to make orange and red ones like this, and Vellrex usually makes blue and purple."

"I sure could use one of those in my bedroom sometimes!" Krikin said. "I wake up to numb toes on the coldest of nights! They tickle so very much when they warm back up!"

Pimsy nodded. "Me, too!"

Niping chuckled. "They're not cheap, and take quite a while to construct. I dare say this one cost just over one hundred books, maybe as many as one hundred and twelve if I remember correctly. Wrote 'em all myself! Took ages. Burned out at least a dozen quills I did. Poor things."

"A hundred and twelve?" Burgundy said, his eyes wide. "That would take me years!"

"Or one cookbook from Jelly!" Binks said, jabbing his good friend playfully.

Jelly giggled and blushed.

The cart climbed and climbed until the snow was falling thick and the forest below vanished in a frozen swirling mist. The tracks before them remained clear, as if the ice either refused to obstruct them or the tracks themselves shooed it away. Soon the trees stopped sliding by, leaving giant boulders and rock faces in their place.

"Mind your heads now," Niping shouted over the howling wind.

Jimmy ducked just as the cart sped through a long, well-lit tunnel. On either side of the tracks, great square windows were carved into the mountains' very stone. Thick frosted glass pulsed with amber light from deep within hidden rooms. Shadows of all sizes could be seen just behind the windows, busy at this or that.

"The first mines. Now they're simply work areas, but just as impressive," Niping explained.

As suddenly as the tunnel appeared, it vanished, and the cart raced further and higher still. They traveled through several more passageways, each well lit and all with windows carved deep into the sides. Once, Jimmy saw a busy elf wave at the cart and its occupants as it zipped by.

"Are there homes here? I mean, inside the mountain?" Jimmy asked.

"Aye, many, lad," Niping replied. "We build our cities within and under the mountains. Dwarves prefer their homes carved from stone and gem. The animals prefer earth and forests, the elves their trees and golden wood, but we dwarves fancy marble, granite, and quartz beneath our feet and over our heads. There are tales of long-lost mountains which still hold entire homes carved out of a single giant ruby, sapphire, or emerald. Some held halls carved out of solid gold or even platinum. In fact, we believe one of these fabled mountains might have been rediscovered in the last few months. As soon as Christmas has passed and our work his is done, we'll send out our experts to explore it."

"Wow. Cities built under mountains. That sounds very nice," Jimmy replied.

Niping looked long and hard at Jimmy and then smiled. "It is, lad, it is."

CHAPTER 26

TREASURES AND DREAMS

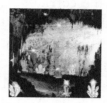

The cart slowed after a time and rolled into an enormous, ice-encrusted cavern. High above, beautiful stalactites hung dozens of feet above equally impressive stalagmites, which reached up towards their ancient inverted cousins. The walls were lined with brass lanterns which burned bright. Each lamp held a large, bright crystal similar to the one Niping had used to warm the cart on its ascent; there were no flames.

"Mind yer step," the dwarf said.

Jimmy and the elves piled out and followed Niping deeper into the cave. He walked over to one of several doorways leading out of the main grotto and pointed to a carving deep in the rock.

"This will lead us to a section of the White River and deep into the forest of Sugar Crystals," Niping said.

"A forest?" Jimmy asked. "Inside a mountain?"

Niping grinned. "Of sorts, lad."

"Oh, I love the sugar crystals," Pimsy said. "I'd build a home out of them if I could!"

Burgundy laughed. "You'd soon be homeless at the rate you go through them, Pimsy."

"Me too!" Krikin said.

Pimsy blushed as the group headed in, Niping leading the way. At first, the tunnel was tight, forcing them to walk in single file, but it didn't take long for the ceiling to rise and the walls to stretch further and further apart. Jimmy was thankful, as he hadn't been able to see much more than Burgundy's bobbing hat just inches from his nose. Eventually, the sounds of picks and various other tools began to echo up the corridor. As the noise grew louder, Jimmy heard music and then singing drifting up the tunnel.

Niping led the troupe around a sharp bend, and Jimmy gasped at what lay before them. The largest cavern he could possibly imagine stretched on and on into the distance. The cave's ceiling was so high it disappeared beyond a haze of shadow - much like the first toy factories had - and along the walls, trails had been cut in an infinite number of switchbacks.

Dwarves and elves by the thousands strolled along, pushing colorful handcarts or carrying equipment. It took several moments, but Jimmy began to notice the walls and floor here were far different than earlier in the tunnels. They were no longer a cool dark gray; this cavern seemed to be cut from pale blue and white ice! Ice so clear it looked like glass. Jimmy glanced down at his feet and began to make out busy figures dashing to and fro far beneath him.

An instant later, a new and cheerful song broke out amongst the miners; they whistled and bobbed, flawless in tune and perfect in step.

There's a magic kind of gift
A treat that's sure to lift
The spirit of a boy or girl
As quick as quick is swift - As quick as quick is swift

Where a heart has fallen low
This gift is sure to go
And mend what's wrong, so sure and strong
The soul is sure to glow - The soul is sure to glow

Fare thee well or fare thee ill
Our treasure's sure to thrill
And place one's smile a million miles
Atop the highest hill - Atop the highest hill

There's a magic kind of gift
Hurrah!
A treat that's sure to lift
Hurrah!
The spirit of a boy or girl
As quick as quick is swift
Hurrah!
As quick as quick is swift
Hurrah!
As quick - as quick - is swift!
HUR-RAH!

"Oh, I love the way their songs echo off the sugar!" Jelly said.

Jimmy glanced back at the walls and then again to his feet. "This is sugar?" he asked, tapping his boot against the floor.

Niping reached over and touched the cavern wall. "The purest and sweetest sugar crystals in the world, lad."

"Just wait, Master Jimmy! You haven't seen anything yet!" Krikin said.

"We're standing on sugar? This, this is all sugar?" Jimmy said.

Niping chuckled and led the group down a long flight of steps, each carved from sugar and lit from beneath.

"Niping!" a voice called out.

The group turned to see a long line of dwarves astride colossal polar bears. At the front of the formation stood the largest of the beasts, and atop him was a white-bearded dwarf with brilliant lavender eyes.

"Did you see the royal?" the dwarf asked, bringing the column to a halt. His smile was broad, sincere, and comforting.

Niping nodded. "I did Róarr, I did. Beautiful specimens, indeed."

"Rumor has it they may have found a second vein in the western tunnels. We're off to see for ourselves."

"A second? So soon?" Niping replied. "Seems a luck-filled year fer certain!"

"Aye, it does." Róarr said and looked over Niping's companions, his amazing eyes settling on Jimmy. "Is this the boy we've been hearing about?"

Jimmy stepped forward and bowed, not knowing the proper response. "Hello, sir."

Róarr let out a long and hearty laugh. "Rise up, lad; ya needn't bow in my presence."

Jimmy straightened himself and tried to look less embarrassed than he felt.

"Come to see our mines, have ya?" Róarr asked.

"Yes sir, they're wonderful," Jimmy replied. "They're like, like something from a dream."

Róarr grinned. "Wondrous dreams, indeed. I like this lad, Niping! Don't go losing him down a far-shaft now."

Niping chuckled. "I'll do my best."

Róarr retrieved a long golden pick which he carried on his back. "Take this with ya, lad; she never misses," he said, and handed the tool to Jimmy.

Jimmy took the pick and found it to be far lighter than it appeared. "Thank you, sir!"

"Just leave her with Niping when you've mined yer fill. He'll know where to find me."

Jimmy bowed again before realizing what he was doing.

Róarr chuckled, as did the rest of the column. "Aye, Nip, I like this lad," Róarr said, winked one lavender eye, and motioned for the column to continue on.

As one of the giant bears passed Jimmy, it seemed to smile and lower its massive head in salute. Jimmy nodded back.

Niping led everyone to a long workbench. This too seemed to be carved from the cave itself, much like the stairs.

"Grab yourselves a pick or two, and we'll be off," the dwarf said.

The elves gathered around the table and sorted through the various paraphernalia. All around them, other miners were too busy singing and working to offer up much conversation.

"I can't believe Róarr loaned you his golden pick!" Krikin said.

Jimmy hefted the instrument in his hands and marveled at the glow covering its surface. "It sure is nice."

"It was the first tool to mine these mountains," Krikin said. "Rumor has it Róarr came with Santa and the first elves to build the North Pole! They helped construct almost everything you've seen so far! I dare say there isn't a single stone in the city's oldest buildings that doesn't have a mark or two on it from that very pick!"

"Wow!"

"Wow is right!" Krikin said, and grinned.

"Let's get a move on, then," Niping said.

The dwarf led the group through the throngs of miners towards the northern part of the grotto. When they came to a tunnel marked with a ring of green lanterns, Niping motioned Jimmy to the front of the group.

"Lead on, lad; I figure yer eyes should be the first to see what lies ahead."

Jimmy stepped forward, and the group followed. The walls

began to close in and change in color the deeper they went. The bluish-white faded behind them, giving way to soft, amber-colored walls. These were lit from within as well, though Jimmy could not see from where; they simply glowed. Not only did the colors change here, but the smell did, too. At first, there was a bit of vanilla in the air, then a more pungent, brown-sugary aroma. The further Jimmy led the group, the more familiar the scent became.

"It's butterscotch!" Jimmy said when he realized what the tunnel was carved from.

"That's right lad! Very good!" Niping replied.

"I told you he'd know," Krikin whispered to the dwarf.

"Up ahead is a small area where we can mine a bit if ya like," Niping said.

Jimmy nodded and led the group onward. After a few yards, the tunnel opened up to a room nearly as large as the ward where Jimmy had spent the last several months. Thoughts of the ward wrenched Jimmy's heart down a bit, but the feeling was short-lived. He hated the constant reminder of the place, but was equally determined not to let it interfere with his adventure. It also helped that the magic of this mountain wouldn't allow gloomy thoughts, it seemed; at least it didn't allow them to take root for very long, and certainly not long enough to sprout and grow.

"If ya look at the walls closely, you'll notice some of the scotch is different than the rest," Niping said. "The clearer it is, the more intense the flavor, although some prefer the cloudier confection for its mellow tones. Personally, I enjoy an even assortment of both."

"And we mine a bit?" Pimsy asked.

"Of course, lass. What's mined is yours."

The group chipped away at the butterscotch, careful to take no more than they could eat or what they intended to give as gifts. Niping found an outcrop to sit on and watched the group with a smile.

"Oh, Alexander will love this," Jelly said. "Butterscotch is his favorite, isn't it?"

Pimsy nodded. "He does love butterscotch in the mornings. Actually he likes it in the afternoon as well. Come to think of it, I've seen him melt it over his dessert in the evenings, too!"

Jimmy chipped some of the intense clear candy as well as some of the opaque treat from the cavern walls. He took special notice of the light emanating from the very walls, ceiling, and floor, and from even the bits of candy he chipped away.

"Niping, where does all of the light come from?"

"I was wondering if ya'd notice that, lad," Niping replied. "We've never been entirely sure, to be honest. Even Vellrex has been at a loss for it, and dragons know almost all there is to know of such flames. That's the best answer I can offer ya, unfortunately. What I can say fer' certain is that once most pieces are collected, they lose their shine after a moment or two. But some, just some, will retain their glow. Those are special candies indeed."

"Santa has a small collection in his house, Master Jimmy," Jelly said. "I'm sure if you ask, he would be happy to show you. I think he reads by its light in the evenings when he doesn't want to disturb the missus or the fire's burned low."

"That would be nice," Jimmy replied. "Reading by sugar-fire."

"Sugar-fire, you say?" Niping said. "I like that. If we have time, there is a display deeper in the mines of just such treasures. But I can't make any promises."

Their bags now a bit less empty, Niping directed Jimmy to another passageway leading deeper into the mines. The tunnels twisted, turned, climbed and fell as they proceeded. Sometimes they would ascend, but more often than not, they plunged deeper into the mountain. On occasion the group would pass other dwarves or elves, busy at work chipping away at the walls or ceiling, sometimes the floor itself. Jimmy spotted numerous bears and reindeer pulling tiny carts loaded with assorted treats. The group passed dozens of side tunnels, some bright, some dark, all leading off to various treasures and wonders. Down each passageway music echoed up from somewhere far below. Eventually Jimmy came to a perfectly round room with several tunnels branching off in different directions.

"Which way?" he asked.

Niping motioned to all of the tunnels and then looked back to Jimmy. "Anywhere ya like, lad. You choose. There's not one that's less impressive than the other if ya ask me."

Jimmy studied the different passages and settled on one which looked older than all the rest and also gave off a scent that gave him an idea. As they started into the tunnel, he heard Krikin whisper something to Niping again but wasn't sure what was said.

This tunnel was soon brighter than the rest, its walls changing from perfectly clear to ruby red and even rainbow-colored before back again. Jimmy was lost in awe when the passageway began to corkscrew down a long twisting staircase carved from cobalt blue candy. From all angles it glowed as bright as Jelly's hair and was just as beautiful. The little elf grinned and her eyes sparkled as they descended the stairwell, its steps worn smooth. When they reached the bottom, an enormous cavern of red and pink stone greeted them.

"I don't think I've ever seen this place," Binks said.

"Me either," Burgundy added.

"I don't think any of you have been here before, my young friends," Niping said.

The roof of the cave was littered in thousands upon thousands of red and pink crystals. The walls appeared to have been polished smooth in places, as had the floor. All about, the cave pulsed with a deep ruby glow.

"Notice the blue streak runnin' out o' the stairwell and across the floor?" Niping asked.

Jimmy looked at his feet, and sure enough, there sat a cobalt blue vein, about a foot wide and running the entire length of the room.

"We followed that blueberry line all the way down here. This was one o' the first mines we dug when the mountain was discovered. Back then, blueberry was difficult to find at best. Highly sought after and closely guarded when found. But when we struck upon the scent of strawberries and cherries we knew we had somethin' special. The blues were hard to locate, but the reds? They were the stuff of legend in those days. It takes an ancient mountain to grow reds and an even older mountain to grow blues alongside it. Taste a piece of blueberry when it's grown next to vein of strawberry or cherry and you'll come to appreciate just how special and how magnificent the gifts from nature can truly be."

Jimmy had never heard of nature growing candy per se, but he understood what the dwarf meant and wished then that he could see what other treasures nature had in store for those who respected it.

"Follow the line over to the wall there, and mine some of the blue. You'll see what I mean," Niping said. "Actually, I think I'll have some myself."

Jimmy and the elves followed their friend over to the cave's far wall. The blue line stretched up to the ceiling, giving the room an appearance of being equally divided.

"It's ok to mine here? What, with the rareness of it all?" Jelly asked. Her hair was pulsing as bright as the blueberry candy before them.

"It is, lass. We've found hundreds o' lines just like this throughout the mountain. This was simply the first," Niping looked over at Jimmy. "Might I borrow ol' True-Gold, lad?"

Jimmy handed over the pick, and Niping took a swing at the

wall. The sound was musical, and a perfect spider web of cracks appeared in the candy. Niping pushed the pick handle upwards, and pieces of the treat fell to the cavern floor. Everyone knelt down to inspect the treasure.

"Notice the smell of it first," the dwarf said.

Everyone picked up a piece and sniffed. Smiles fell over all. "It smells as wonderful as the fruits you elves manage to grow, does it not? Ripe? Sweet? Tangy, even?"

"I wonder if we could grow blueberries that glow like this," Krikin mused.

Jimmy studied the small piece he held and watched as the tiny blue light from within pulsed in his hand.

"Try it while it still has a bit o' glow in it," Niping said.

Jimmy popped the candy into his mouth and was struck at how warm it was.

"It tastes like the candy I had when I was little!" Jimmy said. "I don't know how else to explain it."

The dwarf laughed. "Is there a better kind of sweet? Better than the first candy a child tastes? I think not, lad, so your description could be no more perfect than that."

The elves tried their candy and nodded in agreement.

"I could spend hours in these mines, Master Niping!" Jelly said.

"By the looks o' yer locks, lass, you appear to have already done just that!"

Jelly blushed, and her hair glowed even brighter than the pulsing candy. Niping winked at her and smiled.

Jimmy looked back at the wall. "Niping, I have a friend...back home...and, well...I was wondering if I could take her some of the strawberry? She loves everything to do with strawberries, and I can't think of a better gift than this."

Niping looked to the elves and then back to Jimmy. "Lad, you take whatever ya like."

For the next hour Niping guided Jimmy and the elves to more

wondrous sites. There were grottos of grape, labyrinths of lemon, and waterfalls of watermelon. They saw several workshops where elves and dwarves alike melted, twisted, and shaped various candies into gorgeous designs. They even saw part of a dwarven city. Small homes, taverns, and even a stable or two were all busy with activity. A deep river of pure white liquid cut through the streets in one part of the town. Bridges small and large arched up and over the canal, and occasionally a long wooden boat floated by. Jimmy wished he could see more, but time was running short and before long, Niping led them back to the same spot where they had entered the magical mountain.

As Jimmy climbed into a waiting cart, he turned to face his new friend. "Thank you for letting me tour some of the mines, Niping."

"Not at all, lad," the dwarf replied. "It's always a pleasure to be with someone the first time they see such sights. If ya don't mind, I think I'll ride back down to the harvesting station with you lot."

Of course no one objected, so Niping slid into a seat next to Jimmy and Krikin. Along the way, he told them tales of how the dwarves and elves first discovered some of the treats now bulging within their white bags and of mysterious underground forests where some of the most exotic plant-life you could imagine grew with the help of glowing crystals and luminescent lakes. He described stones which sang, gems that changed in color, and precious metals which could only be molded with dragon-flame.

When they reached the bottom of the slopes, Niping bid them farewell and bowed low to Jimmy, who returned the gesture in kind. Jimmy then gave True-Gold to Niping so he might return it to Róarr with his thanks. Krikin was the first to call his snow skates and send his boots back home to get warm. And though they'd have all liked to remain longer, Jimmy and the elves soon followed suit.

As they skated away, Jimmy spotted Nicodemus and Niping shaking hands and pointing back up towards the mines. Grumble the yeti walked over to both, hoisted them upon his shoulders, and climbed into a waiting cable car. Fenrin circled above, singing loud and clear. The last Jimmy saw of the candy mountain was the cart ascending into the snow-laden clouds, Niping holding the golden pick, and purple fireworks bursting through the silver, snowy haze.

CHAPTER 27

AN OLD FRIEND FINDS AN OLD HOME

J immy and the elves reached the city just as the lanterns in the street sparkled to life and a multitude of windows began to glow for the evening. It had been a wonderful day indeed, and further adventures still lay ahead. Jelly pointed to an enormous red and white striped tower as they glided along.

"Do you remember the Missus telling you that you should ask Krikin about his Flour Tower, Master Jimmy?" she asked.

Krikin spun as he skated and almost sprawled cap over boot. "Oh, she didn't!"

"Oh, but she did!" Jelly replied, and began to giggle.

Krikin regained some of his composure, sighed, and glanced back up to the tower before them.

"Go on, go on Krikin, tell him," Binks urged.

"If you don't, we will!" Burgundy said. He, too, was now giggling.

Jimmy glanced at the nervous elf and smiled. "If it's embarrassing, you don't have to say, Krikin."

"That's precisely why he *should* tell you!" Pimsy said. "If you can't laugh at yourself, who *can* you laugh at?"

Krikin moaned. He paused for a moment, sighed, moaned again, and began. "Well, as it turns out, the Flour Tower was my design a long time ago. You see, we go through so many baking supplies, I thought one central location for basic flour would be a grand idea!"

"And it was, or rather it is," Jelly said.

"Thank you," Krikin replied. "I built the tower as a secret so I could surprise Santa and the Missus, you see. And when it came time to fill it...." Krikin hesitated a moment and looked back up at the tower. "Well, let's just say I was in the wrong place at the wrong time."

Binks began to snicker. "The bottom of the wrong place at the wrong time, to be precise."

"You were inside the tower when it was filled?" Jimmy asked.

Krikin nodded. "I built this amazing balloon to lift the flour up and into the tower, you see. Well, in my haste, I decided to check one of the last traps, and well...I pulled the lever to release the flour, not realizing the door to the tower opened inwards. And, well...."

"It took us three days to find him," Pimsy said, and began to hiccup in a series of gleeful giggles.

Jimmy tried to hide his amusement, but chuckled regardless. "Three days?"

"I swore off baking for a week after that," Krikin replied. "I've never swallowed so much flour in my whole life! I smelled of muffins for a month!"

Jimmy heard a small thud behind him and turned to see Burgundy rolling in the snow. "It took Dasher to get him out! As Santa was away!" he said between gasps for air.

Krikin began to laugh then. "And to make matters worse, I couldn't pop regardless of how hard I tried! You know, like you saw Santa do for Binks earlier?" he said, and looked at Jimmy, who nodded. "I tried and I tried, but I just ended up back inside the flour. So after a while, I just carved out a nice little room and waited for rescue. And waited, and waited, and waited...."

By now everyone was laughing.

"We must have washed his clothes for a week before they stopped making him hungry every single time he put them on," a voice said from ahead.

Jimmy and the elves looked up, and there sat Santa in his magnificent sleigh, the reindeer lined up before him.

Santa continued. "I dare say Krikin has some of the best ideas I've ever seen, but the decision to unleash that flour before he was out of the way...well, that was not one of his finest."

"Santa!" Pimsy said. "Are we leaving so soon? I was hoping to cook something special for Alexander before we left."

A tiny figure climbed out of Santa's pocket and stood upon his left shoulder.

"Ahh, Pimsy," the tiny mouse said. "I wish I could stay longer, but I regret I must leave straight away."

"It is always too soon when a friend leaves," Pimsy replied.

The mouse nodded. "How very, very true."

Elves began to fill the street from every direction. In minutes, an ocean of colorful caps and smiling faces looked towards Santa and his sleigh.

"Farewell, Alexander!" a voice called from the still-growing crowd.

"Aye! Cheers, mate!" another called out.

"And to you all!" Alexander replied. His voice rang out crisp and clear despite his size. "It has been an honor and a privilege to share these few years here with you. I cannot begin to express my gratitude; suffice to say, one could not ask for a better home or truer friends."

Pimsy and Jelly wiped away several tears, as did Krikin.

"We promise to visit whenever we can, Alexander," Krikin said.

The mouse took off his small green and red cap, bowing as he did. "I would be honored."

Santa stood and gazed out over the crowd. "What say we send Alexander off with a little magic?"

The elves all cheered and looked skyward. Jimmy followed their gaze and watched as the clouds above began changing in color. First purple, then blue, followed by green, gold, and silver. A moment later the snowflakes began to change as well. Millions upon millions of brightly colored crystals glided through the air. As they struck the ground, a world of color began to envelop everything. Orange snowflakes landed beside teal and lavender. The icicles hanging from rooftops and tree limbs began to glow and pulse from one color to the next.

Krikin nudged Jimmy. "Not bad for an Elvin version of fireworks, eh?"

Jimmy held out his hand and marveled at the myriad of multicolored flakes there. "It's beautiful!"

"It's like confetti you don't have to clean up!" the elf replied.

As the vibrant display fell, a slow, delicate song flowed to life somewhere within the crowd of elves. It was soft at first, but before long, everyone was singing, even Santa.

Tell your heart not to grieve
True friends never leave
Though their spirit may roam
Our hearts are our home

Remember this carol
Recall this old song
Whenever there's peril
When journeys run long
Tell your eyes not to cry
True friends never fly
Though their travels run long
Our hearts remain strong

So remember this carol
Recall this old song
Whenever there's peril
When journeys run long

Keep our hearts with you friend
Keep our love 'til the end
Keep our laughter and smiles
May they guide you for miles

And remember this carol
Recall this old song
Whenever there's peril
When journeys run long

We will always be with you
We'll always be true
We will never be far
From wherever you are

When the song ended, not a dry eye could be seen blinking up at Alexander and Santa. The crowd was silent at first, and then from somewhere an elf called out.

"Three cheers for Alexander!"

The mass exploded in ovation. "Hip-hip-hurrah!"

"Hip-Hip-Hurrah!"

"HIP-HIP-HURRAH!"

This time, the little mouse wiped away tears of his own. "Thank you all," he managed to say when he cleared the tiny lump in his tiny throat.

Above the street, Vellrex swooped over, billowing blue and purple flames across the sky. The dragon-fire ignited the snow and clouds, sending each flake to earth in a sparkling vibrant glow. Another cheer erupted from the elves, and Vellrex roared.

"You'd think they would never see you again, Alexander," a new voice said.

Jimmy turned to see Mrs. Claus step up to the sleigh, a large basket in her hands.

"Well, I guess we'll have to do something about your favorite cookies," she said, and wiggled her nose. The basket shimmered for a moment then shrank to a minuscule version of itself - just the size for a small mouse to carry.

Alexander took the basket and smiled. "You are too kind, Miss," he said, his voice cracking a bit.

"Not at all, Alexander. I placed the recipe in there as well. I expect you to continue your cooking, you know!"

"Oh I will, I will, I promise."

"Well, off with you, then," Mrs. Claus said, and wiped her eyes in a quick embarrassed motion. "And don't you forget to write!"

Alexander bowed, as he seemed unable to respond verbally.

"Quite right," Santa said, and offered a warm smile to his wife.

"We must be off! And who will come to see Alexander to his new home?"

Every hand within sight shot into the air, and Santa chuckled. He then reached into the rear of the sleigh and untied the giant red sack. One by one the elves jumped up and over the sleigh, disappearing into the magical bag with a 'yippee!' here and a 'woo- hoo!'

there. Within seconds, the sound of music and the smell of baking began to waft out. Alexander bowed one more time to Mrs. Claus, who shooed him away and smiled. Basket in hand, the tiny mouse leapt into the bag and vanished. All that remained were Jimmy and Santa.

"Now you lot be home for dinner!" Mrs. Claus said. She then looked to Santa. "And don't you go off exploring that old house again! You remember what happened last time!"

Santa laughed. "Yes, dear, I remember."

Mrs. Claus wiggled her nose and vanished in a shower of gold and silver light. With that, Jimmy climbed into the sleigh and sat next to Santa.

"Off we go, boys!" Santa called to the reindeer.

Dasher reared, and the team charged off into the night.

CHAPTER 28

A NEW HOME

As they climbed towards the clouds, Jimmy peered down at the places he'd seen and explored throughout the wonderful day. A massive purple firework exploded overhead, and Dasher turned the sleigh to investigate. Jimmy spotted the camp where he'd met Nicodemus, Niping, and the giant yeti so affectionately called Grumble. Hundreds of campfires shimmered now, and far more elves and dwarves rushed about.

Santa waved at several dwarves who spotted them gliding overhead. "Fenrin said they'd unearthed a vein or two of the Royal. Did you get a chance to try any?" he asked.

"No, sir, but I did collect a nice bag of treats for later! And a gift or two."

"A gift or two, eh?" Santa said, and grinned. "Good, good! A shame about the Royal, though perhaps we'll find you some before we leave tomorrow."

"Leave?"

Santa nodded. "I'd like nothing more than to keep you here as long as you'd like, Jim."

Jimmy sighed and lowered his head. "I know. I was just...I was starting to get used to...."

"To what?"

"...to feeling better."

There was a long pause where both remained quiet, and then Jimmy looked up. "I'm afraid to go back, Santa, afraid of being sick again and, and, seeing my parents. How they look when they see me...it's worse than, than being so sick all of the time."

Santa looked down at Jimmy's somber figure and patted his knee. "We still have a lot to talk about, Jim. Why don't you and I have a nice chat after dinner this evening? How does that sound?"

Jimmy nodded.

"Besides, we can't let on to how sad we might be, can we?" Santa added. "Not with Alexander finding his home and embarking on his new life, now can we?"

Jimmy perked up a bit. "No, sir, I guess not."

"He's been searching for his family for quite some time now, you know. While we're all saddened to see him leave, this is a special time for Alexander, a magical time. Let's put on a brave face for his sake, and you and I will discuss troublesome matters with full bellies and steaming cups of cocoa! I promise you will feel better."

Jimmy nodded, and in no time at all, the harsh melancholy weighing him down began to lift. He was still worried at the prospect of returning to the hospital, and he did dread looking into his mother's sad eyes again, but all of those things began to burden him less and less. It was impossible to keep your spirits from rising when Santa promised that everything would be all right.

They soared over vast oceans for several hours. The sky remained clear and the stars brilliant. Jimmy decided to remain in the front of the sleigh with Santa, content to stargaze and dream. The gentle sounds of singing and merriment as well as wonderful aromas drifted out of the colossal red bag, and Jimmy grinned. He caught the scent of gingerbread cookies and specialty drinks wafting from the sack more than once. Dasher spotted pods of beluga whales several times and always descended to get a better look. Santa cheered at the sight of the ghostly mammals and wished them safe travels. Jimmy had seen illustrations of the whales in books, but had no idea how perfectly white they were, or how magical. The North Pole was not the only place in the world that boasted a few delightful and mystical creatures, it seemed.

Soon, the oceans gave way to land, and Santa guided the team east. They soared over snow-covered mountains, endless prairies, and sparkling cities for ages until at last, Dasher began to slow.

"I've always liked Virginia," Santa said as the team reduced speed. "Have you ever been?"

Jimmy shook his head. "I don't think so."

"It can be as enchanting as the North Pole sometimes, from its beaches to its mountains. Oh, the leaves here in the fall are a sight to see, I must admit. Colors you wouldn't believe. It's no wonder so many elves visit this part of the world as often as they do."

Snow began to appear, and far below, the ground faded from bluish-gray to dull white. Just as before, the flakes hung nearly motionless in the air, as time appeared to have been frozen here as well. Jimmy wondered if Santa's magical watch had slowed time for everyone, everywhere, or just people? The beluga whales certainly didn't seem to have been affected.

"It is very pretty," Jimmy said. "It reminds me of home, only with smaller mountains."

Dasher circled for several moments. When he spotted a house not far from a large cluster of buildings, the reindeer began his final descent. Several streets away, a large rooftop came into view, and eventually Jimmy noticed a sprawling brick house surrounded by snow-encrusted trees. The front yard of the home was enclosed by a white picket fence festooned with a frozen army of icicles and decorative red ribbons. A dozen or so stepping stones peeked out from beneath the snow as if they'd been recently swept. The sleigh landed in a clearing just behind the home, and Dasher guided the team to a stop near the rear gate.

Santa and Jimmy climbed out of the sleigh and stood facing the house. "The Henderson home," Santa said. "I've visited countless homes in my time, and none have mystified me quite like this one."

"How do you mean?" Jimmy asked.

"Well, if I were to guess, I'd say it was built by none other than Elvin means. But I have yet to find a single elf who knows anything about it. For example, it's very similar to my magical bag here! It's larger on the inside, though you have to know what you're looking for to see it. Oh, that reminds me," Santa said, and turned to the red velvet sack in the rear of the sleigh and snapped his fingers. It floated up and out, coming to rest without so much as a bump on the fresh snow. A moment later an elf hoped out.

"My, that seemed fast," the elf said. He bowed to Santa and scampered off towards the house.

Eventually most of the elves stood about the sleigh; some built tiny fires, and others conjured fairy lights within the trees. Krikin emerged from the bag, Alexander perched upon his left shoulder. Jelly, Pimsy, Burgundy, and Binks followed not far behind.

"Are you ready, Alexander?" Santa asked.

"If I'm not now, Santa, I'm afraid I never will be!" the mouse replied.

Santa chuckled. "And are the rest of you ready?"

Jimmy and the elves nodded.

"Farewell, Alexander! Until Christmas Eve, old friend!" a voice called out from the multitude of elves.

"Until then!" Alexander called back.

The rest of the elves, save Jimmy and the troup then melted into the tree line, no doubt off to bake away and conjure magical melodies as they were known to do. As the little group neared the rear of the house, Santa snapped his fingers again. One of three doors opened without a sound. Jimmy happened to glance skyward and saw a frozen column of smoke reaching out of the home's brick chimney. For some reason, it appeared friendly, in a way. He couldn't explain why; it just did. The group filed into the Henderson home one by one, Santa leading the way, his magical pocket-watch shining bright.

"It's a very nice kitchen, I must admit," Jelly said as they entered the house. A strong aroma of the family's dinner still hung fresh in the air. The pungent scent of tomato sauce and spicy garlic mixed with oregano and parsley drifted about.

"It sure smells well-loved," Krikin replied. His little tummy growled.

"And well-used!" Binks said in unison with Burgundy and Pimsy.

Santa led them through the kitchen, a small breakfast nook, and a dining room, finally coming to halt next to a long wooden staircase, its banister wrapped in white and green garland.

"The children's rooms," Santa said, and pointed up the stairs. "...and I suspect you might find some of the secrets you've been researching there."

Alexander was unable to speak. He simply smiled.

Santa, Jimmy, and elf alike climbed the stairs and entered a long, cozy hallway. It stretched by several closed doors and ended at the base of yet another set of stairs. The first door on the left stood slightly ajar, and Santa motioned to it.

"Shall we?" Santa asked the still-mute mouse perched upon Krikin's shoulder.

Alexander cleared his throat. "Yes...ahem...yes, please."

Santa opened the door and stepped through.

CHAPTER 29

EVERY HOME HAS A HEART

The children's room was a large one. Jimmy noticed three small beds, a brick fireplace, and an immense, frost-covered window. It reminded him of the guest room he'd been given at the North Pole. While different, the two rooms shared the same comforting and well-loved aura. Jimmy wondered if he'd have a room like this of his own someday.

Several toys littered a maroon and yellow rug, while a handful of pictures, mostly hand-painted, adorned the walls. On the right side of the room's single window, an enormous bookcase stood sentinel over all. It towered floor to ceiling, packed with books of all shape and color.

Pimsy peeked at the tiny sleeping faces. "Oh, it's Michael, Cindy, and Anne!" the elf said. "I was wondering if these were the Hendersons you were speaking about, Santa! But, well, I thought they lived in London?"

"They did, Pimsy. The family moved here just this fall," Santa replied.

"The bombings?" Krikin asked.

Santa nodded.

"Such a horrible thing, wars," Jelly said.

"That they are," Burgundy agreed.

Santa cleared his throat. "Now, Alexander, if you would permit me?" he asked, and held out his hand. Alexander hopped from Krikin's shoulder and onto Santa's mitten. "I think we'd be better suited to continue with a small change," Santa continued. He then placed Alexander on the floor, straightened up and touched a finger to the side of his nose.

Jimmy felt the world disappear and a sensation akin to flying. The soaring feeling morphed into one of falling and, for a moment, Jimmy struggled to comprehend where he was. The room had turned into a blurry mixture of colors, motions and sounds – but just as suddenly as the sensations arrived, they vanished, and Jimmy stood nose to nose with a smiling furry face.

"Aaah!" was the only thing Jimmy managed to say, or rather blurt.

Alexander laughed, and Santa placed a hand on Jimmy's shoulder.

"My apologies, Jim, I should have warned you about that," he said.

Jimmy turned to see the rest of the elves standing about and, in the far, far distance, enormous toys, shoes and furniture towered over the group. A colossal fire roared from what seemed several miles away. Jimmy glanced down at his feet and noticed the burgundy and yellow rug, along with Alexander's feet just a step or two away from his own.

"It's nice to finally meet you face to face, Sir!" the no longer tiny mouse said. "So to speak, that is."

"Alexander…" Jimmy said. "I, I'm sorry I yelled like that."

The mouse laughed and shook his head. "Not to worry, Sir, I dare say I'd have done the same, were I in your shoes. If I wore shoes, that is!"

Jimmy laughed and began to regain his balance.

"I love this point of view. Don't you?" Pimsy asked no one in particular.

"It always makes me think of desserts!" Burgundy replied. "I've never once dived into a pudding, or climbed a frosted cake, but I'm always struck with the inspiration to do just that each time I find myself this size!"

"We might have to address that someday soon, Burgundy," Krikin replied.

"If the missus finds you two swimming about in her chocolate mousse, she's likely to feed you to the polar bears!" Jelly said.

Krikin began to laugh. "Well, we'll just have to inform her of our intentions before that happens, now, won't we?"

"I'd recommend it," Santa said. "Shall we continue?" he added, and motioned towards the bookcase in the distance.

The group began the long trek across the bedroom. Jimmy remained quiet, content to gaze at towering toys and colossal clothing which stretched far above his head. He felt very much as Jack must have felt running about in the giant's castle atop his magical bean stalk. The elves, however, chatted and carried on as if this was nothing new, and Jimmy suspected it wasn't. He'd seen stranger things today.

When they reached the bookcase, Santa motioned Alexander to the far end, near the corner of the room. There, the bookcase stood just far enough from the wall that a tiny mouse - and at the moment, Santa, Jimmy and the elves - could squeeze behind it. They entered the shadowy crevice and walked to the far end, Alexander leading the way, Santa's pocket watch providing just enough light to see.

"Now if you will permit me, Alexander," Santa said. "I would like to give you your Christmas present a bit early."

Jimmy stood behind Burgundy and Krikin, straining to see what Santa handed the mouse. There were several gasps from the elves, while Santa and Alexander spoke in hushed tones. Whatever was being said was meant for Alexander's ears only.

"Santa finally found one of the keys!" Krikin whispered.

"How? Where? I thought they were lost?" Pimsy whispered back.

"Evidently not," Burgundy replied.

"I wonder if he found all of them?" Jelly said.

Just then, the tiny alcove between bookcase and wall was flooded with bright amber light. Alexander had opened a tiny door.

CHAPTER 30

NEW ADVENTURES, OLD SECRETS

"Oh, we finally get to see what's beyond one of the doors!" Krikin said. "I thought we'd never know all of this home's secrets!"

"There are other doors like this one?" Jimmy asked. "I mean tiny ones like this in the house?"

"Three that I know of, Master Jimmy," Krikin replied.

Jimmy wanted to ask more questions, but the group began to file forward. Ahead, Alexander vanished in the golden light, then Santa, followed by Pimsy and Jelly. As he drew closer to the doorway, Jimmy's eyes adjusted, and he noticed a long welcoming hallway extending well into the home's walls, where it appeared to branch off in opposite directions. Dozens of closed doors lined the long hallway on both sides. Krikin, Binks, and Burgundy stepped through the entrance way and Jimmy followed.

The light here was very bright, and it took Jimmy several blinks to coax his eyes into focus. When they did, the first thing he noticed was a very detailed painting of an old, gray-bearded mouse. Below the portrait, the name Alexander Henderson IV had been engraved on a small glass plate. Next to this, another portrait, this one of an ancient-looking man, with an even longer gray beard, sat smiling at passer-bys. His name was simply Zairehl.

"Santa, these are…" Krikin started, and pointed at several glowing orbs floating in the hallway. "These, well, these are fairy lights!"

"Yes, they are, Krikin," Santa replied.

Jimmy hadn't noticed the glowing orbs yet, but now he inspected them more closely. They were just like the fairy lights Krikin used in his garden: soft balls of light, floating about in a warm and pleasant kind of way.

"But…but these lights are…they can't…but…but they are!" was all Krikin managed after that.

"This key will open most of the doors you see here, Alexander," Santa said. "So far, I have counted fifty-seven, of which only five refuse to budge. I suspect there are other keys hidden about the house. I'm sure with a bit of digging you will be able to find them soon enough. But I would suggest starting with this door."

Santa pointed to a beautiful wooden door which had been stained purple and fixed with a red glass knob.

"Here you will find the library and a map of the home. I dare say I wish I had found it sooner! When I first started poking around these old walls I became lost for what seemed days," Santa said, and laughed. "And my knowledge of magic here…well, let us just say it's a bit different, as you will soon discover. Jessica was a little put off, as you can imagine."

Alexander's face was awash in awe. "Santa, I don't…I don't know what to say…."

Santa winked. "Say you will write often and tell us all of the wonders you discover here."

"I will, I promise," the mouse replied.

"Oh, please say we can stay and explore, Santa!" Krikin begged.

Santa began to laugh but shook his head no. "I'm afraid this adventure is for Alexander alone, Krikin, at least for now that is."

Krikin was visibly upset, but nodded. "I hope you find your home and your family, Alexander," he said after a moment. "And you write to me straight away! Don't leave anything out! I want to know everything, you understand! Everything!"

Alexander grinned. "I promise, Sir."

"This is where we part ways, Alexander," Santa said. "We will see each other soon, though, I promise. Oh, and one word of caution. Be careful of the books you read here. Some of them get a bit...overzealous at being read aloud."

"Aloud, you say? I will exercise the utmost caution, then."

Pimsy and Jelly sobbed in great heavy blubbers when they hugged Alexander. Krikin, Binks, and Burgundy were a bit better at hiding their own tears, but a few trickled down their rosy cheeks regardless. When it came time to say his final goodbye, Jimmy cried, too. He tried to shake Alexander's hand, but quickly grabbed the mouse and hugged him tight. Santa tipped his hat and smiled.

When they left, the tiny door closed itself, leaving the group awash in shadows. Alexander stayed behind. Santa led the now-quiet friends back into the bedroom, where he returned everyone to their customary size. The small trek out of the home was almost silent save for a sniff here, a silent sob there, or a heavy hiccup.

As they walked back across the snow-shrouded lawn, Jimmy glanced over his shoulder towards the magical house. He spotted a lone white figure just beyond the light of the elves' fires. It was as tall as a man, round, and wore a black silk hat and scarf. It turned its gaze up to a window on the second floor and waved. Jimmy twisted to ask who it might be, but when he glanced back again, the figure was gone. He could only guess that it was Alexander's friend Nix, bidding his own quiet farewell.

CHAPTER 31

DEAR SANTA

J immy remained in the front of the sleigh on the return trip as well. The elves, save Krikin, had disappeared back inside the magical red sack, content to eat, drink, and merry away the sadness over their friend's departure. Krikin sat nestled between Santa and Jimmy, a veritable fountain of questions, bubbling on and on about the Henderson home. Where had Santa found the key? Did it unlock any of the other doors? Who was Zairehl? Where were the elves? Who conjured the fairy-lights? The inquiries went on and on, with little or no time at all for Santa to reply. Unfortunately, Santa was unable to answer the vast majority of them once given the chance. This only led to the excited elf asking even more and more and more. Santa did not appear to mind, though, and promised they would return as often as possible to learn which new riddles Alexander had found, which he had solved, and which ones still vexed him. This comforted poor little Krikin a bit.

When they touched down at the North Pole again, the town was busier than Jimmy had seen thus far. Every street was now lined with a vast network of conveyor belts, each built from emerald green wood and shining red metal. Along these belts sat thousands and thousands of presents, each beautifully wrapped, complete with bows, ribbons, and tags. No less than a thirty of the giant belts came to an end right in front of Santa's home. As far as Jimmy could see, and down every street he looked, a conveyor belt disappeared towards the great forest and the First Tree, far on the distant horizon.

"Ahh, I see the toy factories are ahead of schedule," Santa said. "I must say, this new present delivery system is quite a sight, Krikin! You dreamt of it, too, you say?"

The elf hopped down from the sleigh and grinned at the conveyor belts around the small town square. "I did, Santa! I thought this would make loading the sleigh a bit easier. Not to mention far, far quicker than before!"

"Well, it looks like it might do just that," Santa replied. "Well done!"

Jimmy grinned. It was nice to see Krikin distracted from the Henderson home and his endless questions regarding it. The mysteries and apparently unanswerable inquiries regarding it not only seemed to perplex the little elf but weighed on him considerably. Krikin bowed towards Santa, excused himself, and scampered off to inspect his newest design.

"I, I will see you at…at breakfast, Master Jimmy!" the elf called out over his shoulder. "Sleep well, and good night!"

"Good night, Krikin," Jimmy called back. He couldn't help but notice the small quiver in the elf's voice and the fact he didn't look back at the sleigh to say good night. It told Jimmy that perhaps Krikin was trying to avoid any further goodbyes right now. He was happy to know how the elf felt, but sad all the same.

Santa placed his magical bag on the snow and thanked the elves who began hopping onto the street one after the other. Jelly,

Pimsy, Binks, and Burgundy all excused themselves, promising to return in the morning as well. Jimmy said goodnight to each while fighting a harsh lump now forming in his throat.

"Let's retreat indoors and get warm," Santa said.

"Okay."

As they walked towards the house, Santa thanked each of his reindeer and the two elves who were busy unfastening them from the sleigh's harnesses.

The Claus living room was warm, cozy and full of wonderful smells, which Jimmy anticipated. It was Santa's home, after all, and expecting anything else would have just been silly.

"Why don't you run on upstairs and change out of those winter clothes? I'll meet you in the kitchen after you've washed up, and we'll see what Mrs. Claus has in store for us tonight," Santa said.

Jimmy nodded and made his way up the stairs. He paused a moment and smiled when he saw Alexander's stocking. When he reached his bedroom, a new fire burned in the hearth, and his Lone Ranger pajamas sat folded on his bed. Jimmy changed and walked over to the window, where he watched thousands of busy elves. The snow was falling again, and this time Jimmy spotted several of the snow people he'd heard of. They looked just as he'd imagined. In fact, he'd built snowmen that looked remarkably similar – that is, back when he was allowed to play in the snow, before he was sick. Jimmy smiled as two of the magical beings glided by, each carrying a present wrapped in colorful fashion. He needed no convincing now that it had been Nix at the Henderson home tonight. As he turned from the window, Jimmy was confronted with several dozen mice staring up at him from the bed.

"Hello?" Jimmy said.

One of the mice stepped forward and bowed. "A pleasure, Sir," the mouse said. His voice was high and tinged with a faint accent.

Jimmy stepped closer. "Are you the house guests Alexander told me about?"

"That we are, Sir. We are hunted in almost every home we find outside of the North Pole, so Santa and the Missus are gracious enough to offer us lodging free from the dangers we so often encounter."

Jimmy thought about that, and swore never to place another mousetrap in his home again, no matter how much his mother begged him to crawl beneath the cabinets to do so. He'd just have to tell her of his new friends, and he was certain she'd understand. If he was ever well enough to leave St. Joseph's, anyway. The thought bit at his heart.

The tiny mouse spoke again. "We just wanted to say hello and offer our thanks for accompanying Mister Alexander to his new home. He was so looking forward to finally going."

"You're welcome," Jimmy replied. "But really, I...I didn't do much."

"You offered your friendship, Sir," another mouse said. "There's no greater gift than that."

"Quite right," one of the other mice said.

Jimmy nodded.

"And that is why we are here, Sir. We came to offer you our friendship as well. If you'll have it," the first mouse said.

"I would love to," Jimmy replied. "Thank you!"

The congregation of mice all bowed in unison.

"If you will excuse us now, Sir, there is quite a bit to see to tonight, as I'm sure you can imagine. Sleep well, and again, thank you for your kindness," the mouse said, and bowed again.

Jimmy wasn't sure how to respond, as he could not think of what he might have done or said to elicit such thoughtful remarks. He simply smiled and watched as the mice disappeared over the side of the bed, off to perform whatever task was required of them.

Santa was already in the kitchen, nestled deep into one of the many chairs about the main table. He wore spectacles now and held a long white quill over an enormous scroll which trailed off the table and disappeared beneath it somewhere. In front of him sat a bottle of red ink into which he dipped the quill, marking the parchment on occasion. Mrs. Claus was placing the last of several forks and spoons at the three settings she'd prepared.

"Did you have a good trip?" she asked as Jimmy walked in.

Jimmy took the seat to which Mrs. Claus motioned. "Yes, Ma'am."

"That's good. Santa tells me you were able to see some of Alexander's new home?"

Jimmy nodded. "Yes, Ma'am, it was very nice. I think he'll be happy there; it was like, like it was built for him."

"I dare say it was, Jim," Santa said.

Mrs. Claus wiped away a small tear. "Oh, I can't believe how much seems gone from this house now. He was such a little fellow to take so much with him!"

"Large hearts require far more room, dear," Santa said. He then snapped his fingers and the parchment, along with the quill and ink, vanished. "Now let's be thankful good ol' Alexander has finally found his home, despite having to leave this one in the process."

Mrs. Claus nodded, and soon the three were treated to another magnificent meal. Honey oatmeal bread and vegetable stew were had all around, and for dessert, a coconut cake with buttercream frosting. Jimmy cleared his bowl, plate, spoon, and fork twice. When the meal was done, Santa excused himself and asked Jimmy to accompany him to the living room. Mrs. Claus sent large mugs of steaming cocoa with them and busied herself with a new cookie recipe.

"Have a seat, Jim," Santa said, and pointed to one of the large wingback chairs in front of the fireplace.

Jimmy climbed into the chair, careful not to spill any of his cocoa. Santa was quiet for a time, content to stare into the fire and sip his drink. Jimmy did the same. He had already guessed at what Santa was going to tell him, and he was more than willing to wait. The longer he could go on believing that this wonderful adventure could last forever, the better. But deep down, he knew it was all going to end, it had to, and he began to feel sorry for Santa at having to admit to what was painfully clear to him already. Jimmy would have to go back. Back to the hospital, back to his sad mother, and back to the sickness which had invaded his body. He felt miserable for Santa and sorry the jolly old man had to break such dismal news to him after he'd shown him such happiness already.

After a while, Santa produced his spectacles and sat his cup of cocoa on a tiny round table between the two chairs.

"I have your letter, here, Jim," Santa began. "I've read over it several times, and I must say, I'm touched."

Jimmy remembered the letter, of course. He'd written it weeks ago, but it had vanished somewhere in the hospital.

"I thought maybe it had gotten thrown away," Jimmy replied.

"Oh no, Krikin was kind enough to bring it here. Once you sign a letter to me, nothing can keep it from arriving." Santa paused for a moment and stared at Jimmy from above his golden spectacles. "You only asked for one thing?"

Jimmy nodded and felt his cheeks flush. "I thought it was the best thing I could give someone."

Santa smiled. "Well, Jim, most children ask for gifts for themselves. It's rare that I receive a request for someone other than the letter's author. Why didn't you ask for something of your own?"

Jimmy looked back at the fire and thought of his letter. "I just thought, well, I thought that everyone I know, they're doing so much for me. My mom, she makes me gifts and reads to me and…

and the doctors, the nurses, they're always bringing me things and taking care of me when...when it gets really bad, or I feel really rotten. So I couldn't think of anything I wanted, and I figured that instead of asking for something that I wouldn't get, I guessed it would be ok to ask for something a little easier to give. Only it wasn't for me."

"What would *you* have asked for, Jim? What wouldn't you get?"

Jimmy's eyes filled with tears, and his voice came in a choked whisper. "To get better."

Santa was quiet again, and Jimmy thought he saw him wipe away tears of his own. "Well, it just so happens that I have another letter here, Jim," he said. "Can you guess who it's from?"

Jimmy dried his eyes and looked over at the letter which Santa held. There, centered on the back of the paper, was a red and pink strawberry drawn in crayon.

"Jenny?" he asked.

Santa nodded. "That is right. The very person you requested a gift for. Would you like to know what *she* wished for?"

Jimmy nodded.

Santa cleared his throat. "Dear Santa," he began. "Thank you so much for the books and toy pony last year! I love them so much! I hope you and Mrs. Claus are doing well and my mommy and daddy say hello too! Also I hope the reindeer are fine! I have had a wonderful summer even though I got really, really sick, but I am getting better and can go home for Christmas I think! My legs don't work like they used to anymore, but that's ok because there are other children I've met who are even sicker than I was. One little boy, his name is Jimmy, has a really rotten time trying to breathe. He coughs so much. I feel sorry for him because he's really nice and his mommy is so pretty, she brings me cookies some-times, but she cries a lot. Jimmy never cries. All I want for Christmas this year is for Jimmy to feel better Santa, so he can go home too, and his mommy can stop crying. Thank You! Love, Jenny."

Jimmy sat stunned, oblivious to the tears now glistening on his cheeks.

"And in your letter," Santa continued. "All you asked for was Jenny to be able to walk again? It seems your letters have quite a bit in common, wouldn't you agree?"

CHAPTER 32

SANTA'S CHRISTMAS WISH

"I never thought... I mean..." Jimmy started and stopped.

Santa placed both of the letters on the table and retrieved his cup of cocoa. "It takes a very, very special occasion for ol' Santa to work this type of old magic, Jim. I wish it occurred more often, I honestly do, but as it happens, I can only grant certain requests once in an extremely long, long while. And even I get a Christmas present each year. That being said, this is one of those times, though you and I need to discuss what exactly that means."

Santa took a sip from his cocoa, allowing the room to fall silent. He watched the fire for a time, and then looked back to Jimmy.

"I would like you to stay here, Jim," he said. "I can grant Jenny's Christmas wish of seeing to it that you get well, but only if you wish to remain here. That must be your decision and your decision alone. I wish there was more I could do, but even I have rules to follow, you know. And let's just say there's someone who's asked me to abide by them, and he lives quite a bit further north than even good Ol' Saint Nick!"

Jimmy's mouth hung open.

"Now before you answer, you must know that I cannot bring your family here. They still have their own lives to live, and that is something I am unable change. So while considering your choice, you must know that regardless of how deeply I wish this were not the case, it is, and over that, I have no power."

Jimmy thought about what Santa was saying and was soon lost in thought.

"I know this is a great deal to consider, Jim, and you do not need to answer now."

Jimmy focused on Santa. "Could I tell them? I mean, can I say goodbye?"

Santa smiled. "Yes Jim, but after that, it would be as if, well, as if they never knew you. Do you understand?"

"They would...they would forget about me?"

Santa nodded. "In a sense, yes. You see, for them to continue their lives, and for me to help in this manner, that is what is required. It is a very difficult decision, Jim; there is no question about it. And know that if you decide that this is what you desire, what is taken from your parents is no small thing, no small thing at all. You must consider this, and consider it well."

Jimmy looked back at the flames within the hearth. "Would they ever, I mean, would we ever see each other again?"

Santa nodded. "Yes, Jim, though that would not be for quite some time."

Jimmy nodded. "I think I understand." He paused for a moment and looked up. "I want them to be happy, Santa. I want my mother to stop crying, to stop being so sad. I want my father to stop worrying. If that means I have to go...to go away, then that's what I want."

Santa nodded. "I have to ask, Jim: are you certain?"

Jimmy cleared his throat and sniffed. "I am. I can't imagine seeing them so sad, so hurt anymore, Santa. Especially if, if it got worse."

Santa nodded again, and the two sat in silence for quite some time. After a while, Santa snapped his fingers, and soft Christmas carols began playing throughout the room.

"You know, Krikin was once faced with a very similar situation. Very, very similar, in fact."

Jimmy looked up. His mind had been on his mother and father and how he might say goodbye to them or even if he would be able to. "He was?"

"Oh yes, most of the elves you see here were once children much like yourself. It has been my pleasure to grant these bitter-sweet wishes over the years. Many a child has come to my home in just such a manner. I only wish I could help more, but even I have limitations."

"Did they know? I mean, did they know you would be able to help me?" Jimmy asked.

"Oh no, no, no. I suspect they had their suspicions, but even I was unsure of my limitations until today. And that is also why you were able to detect their odd reactions towards you at times, those hints of sorrow behind the smiles. Your name whispered on the lips of nearly everyone you met. They have no doubt been hoping that I would be allowed to grant your wish, but as has happened before, I am not always permitted to help. They have learned to prepare themselves for such times. They will no doubt be over-joyed to learn that you will share further adventures with them."

Jimmy smiled. It was a nice thought and his smile was genuine, though his heart ached at the idea of leaving his parents.

"I am sorry, Jim, but I must ask you one last time. Are you quite sure that this is what you wish? Remember, you are also deciding on more than your own future."

Jimmy looked as deep into Santa's eyes as he could, and as far into his own heart as he thought possible. "Yes, Santa. I don't want my parents to hurt anymore. I'll see them again. I can wait."

Santa nodded. "Then you best get a good night's sleep. We have a lengthy trip ahead of us. And remember this, as it is equally important. When you say your goodbyes, when you feel the time is right, or when you need to, all you have to do is snap your fingers."

"Snap my fingers?"

"That's all. It's your magic now, Jim, your decision, and only you can cast this spell. Not I, nor anyone else can do this for you."

Jimmy stood and took a deep breath. He then smiled and threw himself around Santa's neck. The jolly old elf's laughter filled the house as he hugged Jimmy back.

CHAPTER 33

CHRISTMAS EVE

That night Jimmy dreamed of his mother and father. They were wonderful and beautiful dreams. In them, his parents were happy again. They laughed and held one another tight. His father looked young, and his mother's eyes were bright like they used to be. Jimmy woke with a smile on his lips and a tear on his cheek. When he looked outside, it was still dark, and to his surprise, the streets below were empty. After he'd washed and dressed, Santa met him at the foot of the stairs; he was dusted in snow, and his red velvet sack hung over one shoulder.

"I thought I heard you stirring about," Santa said, smiling. Jimmy grinned. "Yes, Sir."

"Everyone else is still asleep, save the Missus and I, oh and the reindeer, of course. They don't sleep much this time of year, you know; too anxious and all that. But you watch! In about..." Santa looked to his pocket watch, and then at the clock on the mantle. "... about fourteen minutes, this place will be a flurry of activity!"

Jimmy laughed. "I thought it would already be busy."

"Oh, we learned a long time ago to get an extra few winks the night before Christmas Eve."

"Well, you two best get in here if you want to avoid the rush!" a voice said from the hallway.

Jimmy and Santa both turned to see Mrs. Claus poking her head around the corner.

"Yes, dear!" Santa replied.

"And good morning, Jimmy," Mrs. Claus said, and then disappeared back around the corner.

Jimmy followed Santa into the kitchen and stopped in his tracks just feet through the door. Before him, the kitchen now stretched further than his eyes could see. Hundreds of long tables surrounded by thousands upon thousands of chairs vanished towards the horizon. The ceiling was now a good seventy to eighty feet high, its long wooden beams wrapped in emerald green holly and multitudes of twinkling white lights. Around the vast room, dozens of wonderfully decorated Christmas trees floated about on invisible wings, and hundreds of new fireplaces burned bright. Music floated by from every direction.

Jimmy ducked as a flurry of red and green plates zipped overhead and began placing themselves at seat after seat. Gold utensils fluttered by as well, spreading out in all directions, followed by multitudes of steaming bread baskets.

"We like to serve breakfast to everyone on Christmas Eve," Santa said. "It's a tradition we started long ago."

"Wow."

"And there you go with that word again," Santa said, and laughed.

Jimmy noticed that while always somewhat cheerful, Santa was the epitome of merriment today.

"You two grab your seats, and I'll see to it you're not forgotten in the rush," Mrs. Claus said.

"Come on, Jim, she means business today!" Santa said. They raced to a couple of seats nearest them.

Soon a soft murmur began to echo through the enormous

room. Jimmy watched as elves, dwarves, even snow people appeared from all directions. Several polar bears lumbered by, and even a reindeer or two zipped overhead.

"So everyone comes for breakfast on Christmas Eve?" Jimmy asked. "Everyone?"

"That they do! Oh, we do this several times throughout the year if we can, but Christmas Eve breakfast is always something special. Mrs. Claus looks forward to and plans for it all year long. She never disappoints."

Soon the entire kitchen was filled, at least from what Jimmy could see. The room was so big he still had a hard time comprehending how far it actually extended; he guessed there could easily be a million hungry bellies at the tables now. Santa stood at last and raised a hand. The room fell quiet.

"Thank you all," he began. "I would like to start this year by telling you again how much I admire and cherish each one of you. You are my closest friends and in saying that, you are my family. Each day I find myself learning something new! That is in no small part due to the lessons each of you has taught and continue to teach. So again, I thank you, from the bottom of my heart. Now, it is my pleasure this year to introduce you to a very special young man and newest North Pole resident! Master Jim, if you will," Santa said, and motioned for Jimmy to stand.

Jimmy's face caught fire as he stood and burned cherry-bright as an explosion of cheers erupted throughout the giant hall.

"I know you will all be more than willing to assist young Jim here and teach him some of the many magical lessons you have shown me over the years."

Another wave of cheers broke out.

"To Santa and Master Jimmy!" an elf called out.

"Hip-hip-hurrah!"

"Hip-Hip-Hurrah!"

"HIP-HIP-HURRAH!"

Jimmy laughed and waved at the multitude.

"Now, on to another, no less important matter," Santa said. "Breakfast!"

Another round of applause was followed by a moment of silence. When Jimmy looked back up, an army of serving utensils and containers filled the air from every direction. Steaming cinnamon buns with bits of apples and raisins were served. Hotcakes with toffee and caramel drifted by. Eggs, rolls, fruits, cakes, the list went on and on and on. No belly went unstuffed, and no mouth unpleased.

Krikin and Pimsy stopped by at one point, each grinning from ear to ear. Jelly, Binks, and Burgundy found their way to Santa and Jimmy as well, each equally as happy and vibrant. Nicodemus and his yeti friend Grumble waved to the two from a distance away, Nicodemus astride the giant's shoulder. It was a wonderful time.

"Well, Jim, you and I have a spot of business to take care of before we embark on tonight's big trip," Santa said at last. "Are you ready?"

"Yes, Sir," Jimmy replied.

Santa grinned and looked over to Mrs. Claus and waved. She smiled, blew him a kiss and winked to Jimmy.

"Let's be off then. And take this," Santa said, and handed Jimmy a small brown basket. "Some of the cookies you baked on your trip here. We'll need them."

Jimmy took the basket, and Santa snapped his fingers.

Jimmy blinked, and in an instant, he was sitting in Santa's sleigh, Dasher and the rest of the reindeer already fastened in and rearing to go.

"If you will, boys!" Santa called to his reindeer.

The sleigh jolted forward and was high above the city within seconds. After a short time, the clouds parted, and an endless sea of dark waves glistened up at the sleigh from far below. Jimmy wasn't sure, but he thought the reindeer were flying especially fast this time. It certainly seemed that Dasher and the rest were working harder than he'd seen them work before. Jimmy watched as the moonlight danced and glittered on the surface of the ocean. He knew what was to come, he understood why, and he was confident in his decision, but it didn't help keep the tears from showing up every so often. He wished the reindeer would slow down just a little.

The sea soon gave way to shadowy hills and mountains after a time, and finally dark outlines of moonlit cities raced by far below. Dasher slowed the team and descended towards the faint rooftops. Everywhere Jimmy looked, the buildings were black. Not a single light shined anywhere, not even in the streets.

"It's so, so dark here," Jimmy said.

"That's because we're over England at the moment," Santa replied. "They have to keep the cities dark for fear of the bombers above."

"We're in England?" Jimmy asked.

Santa nodded, and the expression on his face grew sad.

"You should see the city on a night without the fear of war in the air, Jim. It's a splendid sight," Santa said.

Just then, Dasher guided the sleigh over an entire area of broken and burnt structures. Buildings lay on their sides in places, and smoldered in ruins in others. The landscape could not have looked less like the North Pole. After a time, the ground gave way to more ocean, and Dasher sped on. When he reached a long, battered-looking coast, he reared skywards and began circling over an enormous forest.

"Take us in, if you please, my friends," Santa asked.

The sleigh glided through the canopy of trees and landed on a bed of ice and snow.

"I must ask you to stay here, Jim. There is something I need to do, and some things are better left unseen by eyes as young as yours if it can be helped."

Jimmy nodded, though all he could see were dark trees and snow-encrusted brush. Santa stepped off of the sleigh and disappeared into the forest. Blitzen glanced over his shoulder and nodded as if to tell Jimmy everything would be okay. The forest was still, and Jimmy found himself staring at the snowflakes suspended in midair all about him. After a long, long while, the quiet was broken by the crunching sounds of frozen footsteps approaching. As they grew closer, voices began to drift out of the shadows, and two shapes emerged. This time, Jimmy could not keep the tears away.

CHAPTER 34

GIFTS

At the sight of his son sitting in Santa's sleigh, Mark Peterson burst into a desperate sprint. Jimmy scarcely had time to comprehend who he was seeing before he was heaved up and out of the sleigh by strong and loving arms.

"Jimmy! My boy Jimmy!" his father shouted.

"Dad?" Jimmy gasped between sobs. "Dad, it's you, it's really you!"

Jimmy stared at his father in disbelief. He'd seen Santa, elves, dragons, dwarves, talking mice, and fairies over the last two days - he'd even seen living snowmen, a yeti, and dancing quills - but the sight of his father was so magical, so special, that it was almost impossible to believe. His father looked tired and frightened. An enormous bandage covered half of his head, and Jimmy realized a sling had been holding one of his arms until his father ripped it free to hoist Jimmy out of the sleigh and hug him.

"Oh thank you, God, thank you!" Jimmy's father cried, and fell to his knees, still holding his son tight. His chest heaved with deep sobs. "I've been trying to get home Jimmy, I have! They sent for me weeks ago and then we were cut off and then...."

"It's okay, Dad, it's okay!" Jimmy said, and hugged his father as hard as he could.

"Is this really happening? Are you really here? Is this real?" Jimmy's father asked.

"Oh, I assure you it's real," Santa replied.

Jimmy's father looked up and climbed to his feet, still clutching his son tight. He groaned at invisible pains which were not easily ignored.

"I'm sorry it took so long, Mark," Santa said. "I've had Krymson out looking for you for quite some time now."

"Krymson?" Jimmy's father asked.

"Vellrex's brother; he's a dragon!" Jimmy replied.

"A dragon?"

Santa chuckled. "Forgive me; I'm just excited to finally find you. Shall we be going?"

Mark looked at the sleigh. "I don't understand."

Santa placed his hand on Mark's shoulder. "I think you've had enough war for one life, and this war has had enough of you, as far as I'm concerned."

Jimmy's father cried then. He hugged his son close with one arm, and Santa with the other. No amount of broken bones or bruises could have stopped him.

"But my men, I..."

"They'll be just fine, Mark. I promise," Santa said. "Krymson is watching over the entire unit now. He won't let anything happen to them."

"It's okay, Dad!"

"I just have one more stop, if you don't mind," Santa said. "And I was wondering if you could help me with that, Mark?"

Jimmy's father smiled. "I don't believe this is happening, but, but you brought me to my son. I'll do anything you ask, Sir."

Santa smiled. "Oh, this is no dream, Mark. And please, call me Santa."

"Yes, Sir…I mean…Santa."

Everyone laughed.

Santa and Jimmy helped Mark into the sleigh and wrapped him in a thick blanket.

"My men? A dragon… A dragon is guarding them?" Mark asked when he was seated.

"He is! And they will be fine; cold for a bit longer, but fine. Young George is less than a day away," Santa replied.

"George? Patton? George Patton? The Thirty-Seventh is this close? So soon?"

"That he is Mark, that he is," Santa replied. "By the way, you should try one of Jim's cookies. Now, if you will please, Dasher!"

Dasher reared and charged forward. The sleigh jumped, and in the spark of a second, shot into the air.

When Jimmy's father caught his breath he looked over the edge of the sleigh, laughed, and then turned to his son. "Cookies, you say?"

Jimmy reached down into the basket Santa had given him. He retrieved one of his gingerbread cookies and handed it to his father.

"I made 'em with the elves!" Jimmy said.

"Did you now?" his father replied, and took an eager bite. He smiled, but tears streamed from his eyes as he did.

Santa looked over to Jimmy and his father. "I think you'll feel better by the time you finish that, or my name's not Saint Nick!"

"He's right," Jimmy said. "Santa knows his cookies."

Jimmy rested his head on his father's arm and tried to be strong. He loved his father very much, and he would stay with him forever if he could, but that just wasn't possible. He knew this, and he knew he needed to say goodbye very soon, but it was still painful no matter how right he knew his decision to be.

Dasher guided the team higher and higher until finally he

leveled off. When Jimmy's father finished his cookie, he moved his once-bandaged arm about and grinned.

Santa noticed and chuckled. "I told you!"

Jimmy's father laughed. "Yes, Sir, you sure did."

Eventually the sleigh glided over a new city. This area was dark, just as England had been, though the buildings here were not in such dire shape.

"Germany?" Jimmy's father asked.

Santa nodded. "Germany."

After a few minutes, Dasher landed the sleigh on a giant rooftop. Santa reached behind him and retrieved his red bag. "If you please," he said, and motioned for Jimmy and his father to follow.

They crossed the roof and found a door, which Santa opened. The three made their way down a small set of stairs and turned onto a long, ornate hallway. The interior of the building was brightly lit, and soldiers stood guard at almost every turn. Red, black, and white flags hung on wall after wall.

"They can't see or hear us, Mark," Santa said, and began counting doors as he passed. When he found the one he was looking for, Santa opened it and motioned Jimmy and his father to enter. The room was dark, lit only by a small fading fire which now stood frozen in time. It cast just enough light over the room for Jimmy to notice an ornate four poster bed, long maroon drapes covering whomever slumbered there.

"Whose house is this?" Jimmy's father asked.

"Oh, I think you know," Santa said. He walked towards the fireplace, where two stockings hung from silver hooks.

"Would you do me the honor, Mark?" Santa asked and reached inside his bag. He withdrew the pitch-black present Jimmy had seen him take from the workshop below the First Tree yesterday. He untied the ebony ribbon and produced a large and sad-looking piece of coal. He turned it over in his hand and handed it to Jimmy's father.

Jimmy's eyes widened as his father grinned. The stockings were almost identical save one initial each. A large red 'A' and a similar 'E' were the only differences between them. Mark reached for the one adorned with an 'A'.

"It would be my pleasure," Jimmy's father said, and dropped the coal into the sock.

"*That* will cause quite a stir," Santa said.

CHAPTER 35

HOME FOR THE HOLIDAYS

S anta, Jimmy, and his father traveled for what seemed hours after that. Jimmy knew they were heading towards St. Joseph's. He also knew that the team could fly far faster than they were now going, and he silently thanked Santa and the reindeer for all of the precious moments they could gift him. By the time they reached the hospital, Jimmy thought his father couldn't have been in better spirits. When they entered the children's ward, Jimmy realized he was wrong. His father raced across the floor and lifted his mother from her chair in one graceful move. To Jimmy's surprise, his mother woke and stared in shock at her husband.

"Mark?" she asked. "Am I...."

"Hi, honey!" Jimmy's father replied. "No, you're not dreaming. I may be! But you're not!"

The two kissed after that and held each other tight. When Jimmy's father placed her gently on her feet, she wiped the tears from her eyes, and spotted Jimmy standing next to Santa.

"Jimmy?" she started, but her knees wilted beneath her.

"Whoa there, sweetheart," Jimmy's father said, and half-carried, half-guided his wife back into her chair by the window.

"What's happening?" she asked.

"Hello, Susie," Santa said. "It's been a very long time."

Jimmy's mother stared at Santa for several seconds, and more tears began to stream from her eyes. A memory from long ago, since faded over time, resurfaced. "Santa?" she asked in a tiny whimper. "Is it really you?"

Santa snapped his fingers, and the room was filled with colored lights, decorations and enchanting music. Two new Christmas trees stood at each end of the ward, surrounded by multitudes of gifts.

"I promised we'd see each other again someday, didn't I?" Santa said.

Jimmy's mother looked around the newly decorated room, her eyes wide, and her jaw agape. "I thought...I thought you were a dream."

"Oh no, not really," Santa said. "I'm quite real. At least I hope so!"

Jimmy stepped towards his parents. "Santa told me you used to bake hazelnut cookies?"

Jimmy's mother tore her eyes from Santa and smiled at her son. "I did. I mean, when you were very little I did."

"Well, the elves and I miss them quite a lot," Santa said. "The missus is keen to learn your recipe, but don't tell her I told you. So you must do us all a favor and start baking them again posthaste!"

Jimmy's mother nodded and held her arms towards her son. Jimmy ran forward and was wrapped in both his mother's embrace as well as his father's. The feeling was love made tangible.

Before he wanted to, Jimmy pulled away and looked at his parents. "I have to go," he said.

It wasn't what he had intended, or how he had imagined leaving, but such things rarely go as planned.

"What do you mean, sweetie?" his mother asked.

"Go where, Jimbo?" his father added.

"I'm not, I mean, I can't...." Jimmy's voice broke, and he started again. "I can't get better here. You both know how sick I am, even if, even if you never told me. I mean, I know why you didn't. It's just...I can't stay here, and...." Jimmy could say no more. His throat closed up, and for the first time ever, he cried in the children's ward.

"What young Jim here is trying to say is, I've offered him a new home where he can get well," Santa said.

Jimmy's parents looked up at Santa, their faces blank.

"I have to go with Santa, or I won't get better...and, and neither will you!" Jimmy said. He wiped his eyes with the sleeve of his coat and put on the bravest face he could. "But, but we'll see each other again someday!"

"Can we?" his mother said, and stopped, her voice catching deep in her throat.

"I wish you could, Susie," Santa said. "I really do. But I can only take young Jim here."

"But," Mark began, and he too had to pause and clear his throat. "But, he'll get better? I mean, he won't...."

"No Mark, he won't," Santa said. "Not for a very, very, very long time."

Jimmy did not need either of them to explain what the unsaid words were. He knew deep down.

"He'll be as healthy as you see him now. Those horrible coughs are a thing of the past, I promise," Santa said.

"I met lots of new friends. I wish I could show you," Jimmy said. "You would, you would really like Krikin...and Pimsy...and... Jell...." Jimmy could say no more. He wiped more tears from his eyes and snapped his fingers.

The world froze and was bathed in silver light. There was a soft ringing of bells, and the room came back into focus. Jimmy's father was no longer standing next to his mother; he lay sleeping in a hospital bed which resembled the one Jimmy had occupied for so long. Beside him, Jimmy's mother slept peacefully, a small smile resting on her lips. Next to the bed stood a small Christmas tree. It held a tiny string or two of lights and half a dozen ornaments.

Jimmy turned and inspected the room. The children had vanished, and now men of all ages slept. The nurse's station had changed in size and location.

"Santa?" Jimmy asked.

"I'm here, Jim," came a soft reply. "We are still in St. Joseph's, albeit a different wing which was added on after the war began. This place is reserved for soldiers returning from the war. Your father is home safe, and your mother is tending to him, as are the doctors and nurses here. He'll be just fine."

Jimmy walked over to his parents. "So, they, they don't, I mean, they can't remember me anymore."

Santa placed a hand on Jimmy's shoulder. "No, Jim. They won't for a good long time."

Jimmy nodded and kissed his father's cheek. He then leaned over and hugged his mother tight. "I'm okay," he whispered in her ear. "I'll visit you every Christmas Eve, I promise."

"*Are* you okay, Jim?" Santa asked.

Jimmy looked up and smiled. "She looks so happy."

"She'll always love you, Jim. So will your father. Love is a funny thing; it ignores time and space, and even if they don't remember you, they'll still dream of a little blonde boy with sparkling eyes and a brilliant smile. And in those dreams, they will love and watch over you. And I promise, you will all meet again and have grand adventures before you know it," Santa said.

Jimmy hugged Santa and smiled. "Thank you, Santa."

"Thank *you*, Jim. Now, do you still have that gift for young Jenny?"

Jimmy reached into his coat and withdrew the white bag

Niping had given him. He opened it and sniffed the air as a pungent wave of strawberry burst forth. "Yes, Sir!"

"Well, let's make sure she gets it, shall we?" Santa asked.

Jimmy and Santa made their way back through the hospital to the children's ward and found the little girl sitting in bed coloring. Jimmy froze when he saw that she was not stationary with the rest of the children. He looked at Santa.

"Can she see us?" he asked.

"Well, I think she can, by George," Santa said, and began to chuckle.

Jimmy looked back towards Jenny, who was now transfixed on the two, an enormous smile spreading across her face.

"Santa!" she said.

"Hello, Jenny," Santa replied.

Jenny held out her arms, beckoning a hug, as her legs now prevented her from leaping off the bed and racing across the ward - something Jimmy suspected she would have done had she the means.

Santa walked over and engulfed the little girl in a giant hug. "I've brought along a friend," he said, and pointed to Jimmy.

"Are you an elf?" Jenny asked. "You look sort of familiar."

Jimmy thought about that for a moment and then nodded. "I think so!"

"I've never met an elf before," Jenny replied. "I met Santa in a parade last year. You look happier this time!" she said to Santa.

"I do? Well, it is Christmas Eve, you know! I'd hope I looked happy!"

"Oh, I know!" Jenny replied. "Did you get my letter? About the...." Jenny stopped and blinked for a moment. She shook her head, and looked back to Jimmy. "You're Jim! I mean Jimmy! You used to be in...." She stopped and looked over to the bed where Jimmy should have been. "Santa, you DID get my letter! Are you feeling better, Jimmy?"

Santa did not try to hide the surprised expression which washed over his face; he simply laughed.

"I am, Jenny, and thank you!" Jimmy replied.

"You're welcome," the little girl said. "I knew you would get it!" she added, and looked back to Santa.

"I get all letters addressed to me, Jenny," Santa said.

"Jenny, I...I brought you something from the North Pole. I hope you like it," Jimmy said. He stepped closer and handed Jenny the small white bag.

The little girl opened her gift, and her eyes grew wide. "It smells like strawberries!"

"It's strawberry candy, from the candy mines," Jimmy replied. "I found it in a giant mountain made of the most wonderful candies you could ever imagine!"

Jenny reached in and retrieved a piece of the ruby red and pleasantly pink treat. She held it up, sniffed it, and popped the candy into her mouth. Her eyes widened even more after that.

"It twastes juwst wike stwaw-bewies!" she said, and began to laugh, She then slurped up a river of drool before it cascaded over her chin, and giggled.

"I'm glad you like it."

Jenny laughed and held her arms out for Jimmy to come closer, which he did. The little girl hugged him snug.

"I'm not going to remember you after tonight, am I?" Jenny asked.

Jimmy straightened and glanced to Santa. "I umm, I don't think so, Jenny."

"That's okay, I'm just glad you're better."

Jimmy smiled. "Me too, and thank you again, Jenny."

"Well, we better be off, young miss." Santa said.

The little girl smiled and began to giggle. "Merry Christmas, Santa!" she said and continued to laugh.

"And to you."

Jenny looked back at Jimmy again, her laughter becoming almost uncontrollable. "And merry Christmas, Jimmy. I'm sorry I won't remember you!" she said, her laughter coming in waves now.

"Me too," Jimmy replied. The little girl's laughs were making him snicker now. "What's so funny?" he asked.

Jenny held her stomach and tried to reply between gales of giggles. "It's th-this... this straw-strawberry can-candy! It's so...it's so good, it's tickling my feet! My toes tickle so much!" she replied, and bowled over, lost in wondrous mirth.

Jimmy looked to Santa, who winked back at him. "Merry Christmas, Jenny," Jimmy said.

CHAPTER 36

MERRY CHRISTMAS

S anta and Jimmy made their way back to the roof, where they found the reindeer ready and eager as always.

"So would you like to accompany the elves and I tonight, Jim?" Santa asked as the two climbed into the sleigh.

"Yes, please!" Jimmy replied.

"Good, good. Now why don't you pour us both a cup of hot cocoa and let's see if we can't get this sleigh loaded and ready in time?" Santa replied, a wonderful smile covering his face. He pressed a silver button on the front of the sleigh, and two cups slid out of a hidden compartment. A second later, a tall carafe moved into place. The smell of cocoa filled the night air.

Jimmy grinned and set to work preparing his and Santa's hot chocolate. He was eager to return and see his friends again, as well as help deliver gifts to the children of the world. As the sleigh climbed into the night, he thought of his parents and what surprises he could leave beneath their little tree.

~The End~

Made in the USA
Coppell, TX
27 November 2023

24841194R00132